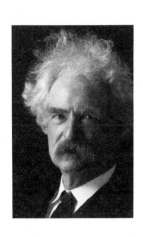

THE DIARIES OF
ADAM AND EVE

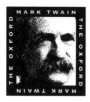

THE OXFORD MARK TWAIN

Shelley Fisher Fishkin, Editor

The Celebrated Jumping Frog of Calaveras County, and Other Sketches
 Introduction: Roy Blount Jr.
 Afterword: Richard Bucci

The Innocents Abroad
 Introduction: Mordecai Richler
 Afterword: David E. E. Sloane

Roughing It
 Introduction: George Plimpton
 Afterword: Henry B. Wonham

The Gilded Age
 Introduction: Ward Just
 Afterword: Gregg Camfield

Sketches, New and Old
 Introduction: Lee Smith
 Afterword: Sherwood Cummings

The Adventures of Tom Sawyer
 Introduction: E. L. Doctorow
 Afterword: Albert E. Stone

A Tramp Abroad
 Introduction: Russell Banks
 Afterword: James S. Leonard

The Diaries of Adam and Eve

Mark Twain

FOREWORD

SHELLEY FISHER FISHKIN

INTRODUCTION

URSULA K. LE GUIN

AFTERWORD

LAURA E. SKANDERA-TROMBLEY

New York   Oxford

OXFORD UNIVERSITY PRESS

1996

OXFORD UNIVERSITY PRESS

Oxford   New York

Athens, Auckland, Bangkok, Bogotá, Bombay
Buenos Aires, Calcutta, Cape Town, Dar es Salaam
Delhi, Florence, Hong Kong, Istanbul, Karachi
Kuala Lumpur, Madras, Madrid, Melbourne
Mexico City, Nairobi, Paris, Singapore
Taipei, Tokyo, Toronto
and associated companies in
Berlin, Ibadan

Published by
Oxford University Press, Inc.
198 Madison Avenue, New York,
New York 10016

Oxford is a registered trademark of
Oxford University Press

Library of Congress
Cataloging-in-Publication Data

Twain, Mark, 1835–1910.
[Extracts from Adam's diary]
The diaries of Adam and Eve / by Mark Twain; with
an introduction by Ursula K. LeGuin and an
afterword by Laura E. Skandera-Trombley.
p. cm. — (The Oxford Mark Twain)
Includes bibliographical references (p.).
Contents: Extracts from Adam's diary (1904) —
Eve's diary (1906).
I. Twain, Mark, 1835–1910. Eve's diary. II. Title.
III. Title: Eve's diary. IV. Series: Twain, Mark,
1835–1910. Works. 1996.
PS1309 1996b
813'.4—dc20
96-14732
CIP
ISBN 0-19-510152-9 (trade ed.)
ISBN 0-19-511422-1 (lib. ed.)
ISBN 0-19-509088-8 (trade ed. set)
ISBN 0-19-511345-4 (lib. ed. set)

9 8 7 6 5 4 3 2 1

Printed in the United States of America
on acid-free paper

FRONTISPIECE
Samuel L. Clemens appears here in a photograph
taken by Joseph Gaylord Gessford in 1904, the year
Clemens published "Extracts from Adam's Diary."
(The Mark Twain House, Hartford, Connecticut)

CONTENTS

EDITOR'S NOTE

The Oxford Mark Twain consists of twenty-nine volumes of facsimiles of the first American editions of Mark Twain's works, with an editor's foreword, new introductions, afterwords, notes on the texts, and essays on the illustrations in volumes with artwork. The facsimiles have been reproduced from the originals unaltered, except that blank pages in the front and back of the books have been omitted, and any seriously damaged or missing pages have been replaced by pages from other first editions (as indicated in the notes on the texts).

In the foreword, introduction, afterword, and essays on the illustrations, the titles of Mark Twain's works have been capitalized according to modern conventions, as have the names of characters (except where otherwise indicated). In the case of discrepancies between the title of a short story, essay, or sketch as it appears in the original table of contents and as it appears on its own title page, the title page has been followed. The parenthetical numbers in the introduction, afterwords, and illustration essays are page references to the facsimiles.

FOREWORD

Shelley Fisher Fishkin

S amuel Clemens entered the world and left it with Halley's
Comet, little dreaming that generations hence Halley's
Comet would be less famous than Mark Twain. He has been
called the American Cervantes, our Homer, our Tolstoy, our
Shakespeare, our Rabelais. Ernest Hemingway maintained that "all modern
American literature comes from one book by Mark Twain called *Huckleberry
Finn.*" President Franklin Delano Roosevelt got the phrase "New Deal" from
A Connecticut Yankee in King Arthur's Court. The Gilded Age gave an entire
era its name. "The future historian of America," wrote George Bernard Shaw
to Samuel Clemens, "will find your works as indispensable to him as a French
historian finds the political tracts of Voltaire."[1]

There is a Mark Twain Bank in St. Louis, a Mark Twain Diner in Jackson
Heights, New York, a Mark Twain Smoke Shop in Lakeland, Florida. There
are Mark Twain Elementary Schools in Albuquerque, Dayton, Seattle, and
Sioux Falls. Mark Twain's image peers at us from advertisements for Bass Ale
(his drink of choice was Scotch), for a gas company in Tennessee, a hotel in
the nation's capital, a cemetery in California.

Ubiquitous though his name and image may be, Mark Twain is in no
danger of becoming a petrified icon. On the contrary: Mark Twain lives.
Huckleberry Finn is "the most taught novel, most taught long work, and most
taught piece of American literature" in American schools from junior high to
the graduate level.[2] Hundreds of Twain impersonators appear in theaters,
trade shows, and shopping centers in every region of the country.[3] Scholars
publish hundreds of articles as well as books about Twain every year, and he

is the subject of daily exchanges on the Internet. A journalist somewhere in the world finds a reason to quote Twain just about every day. Television series such as *Bonanza, Star Trek: The Next Generation,* and *Cheers* broadcast episodes that feature Mark Twain as a character. Hollywood screenwriters regularly produce movies inspired by his works, and writers of mysteries and science fiction continue to weave him into their plots.[4]

A century after the American Revolution sent shock waves throughout Europe, it took Mark Twain to explain to Europeans and to his countrymen alike what that revolution had wrought. He probed the significance of this new land and its new citizens, and identified what it was in the Old World that America abolished and rejected. The founding fathers had thought through the political dimensions of making a new society; Mark Twain took on the challenge of interpreting the social and cultural life of the United States for those outside its borders as well as for those who were living the changes he discerned.

Americans may have constructed a new society in the eighteenth century, but they articulated what they had done in voices that were largely inter-changeable with those of Englishmen until well into the nineteenth century. Mark Twain became the voice of the new land, the leading translator of what and who the "American" was — and, to a large extent, is. Frances Trollope's *Domestic Manners of the Americans,* a best-seller in England, Hector St. John de Crèvecoeur's *Letters from an American Farmer,* and Tocqueville's *Democracy in America* all tried to explain America to Europeans. But Twain did more than that: he allowed European readers to *experience* this strange "new world." And he gave his countrymen the tools to do two things they had not quite had the confidence to do before. He helped them stand before the cultural icons of the Old World unembarrassed, unashamed of America's lack of palaces and shrines, proud of its brash practicality and bold inventiveness, unafraid to reject European models of "civilization" as tainted or corrupt. And he also helped them recognize their own insularity, boorishness, arrogance, or ignorance, and laugh at it — the first step toward transcending it and becoming more "civilized," in the best European sense of the word.

Twain often strikes us as more a creature of our time than of his. He appreciated the importance and the complexity of mass tourism and public relations, fields that would come into their own in the twentieth century but were only fledgling enterprises in the nineteenth. He explored the liberating potential of humor and the dynamics of friendship, parenting, and marriage. He narrowed the gap between "popular" and "high" culture, and he meditated on the enigmas of personal and national identity. Indeed, it would be difficult to find an issue on the horizon today that Twain did not touch on somewhere in his work. Heredity versus environment? Animal rights? The boundaries of gender? The place of black voices in the cultural heritage of the United States? Twain was there.

With startling prescience and characteristic grace and wit, he zeroed in on many of the key challenges — political, social, and technological — that would face his country and the world for the next hundred years: the challenge of race relations in a society founded on both chattel slavery and ideals of equality, and the intractable problem of racism in American life; the potential of new technologies to transform our lives in ways that can be both exhilarating and terrifying — as well as unpredictable; the problem of imperialism and the difficulties entailed in getting rid of it. But he never lost sight of the most basic challenge of all: each man or woman's struggle for integrity in the face of the seductions of power, status, and material things.

Mark Twain's unerring sense of the right word and not its second cousin taught people to pay attention when he spoke, in person or in print. He said things that were smart and things that were wise, and he said them incomparably well. He defined the rhythms of our prose and the contours of our moral map. He saw our best and our worst, our extravagant promise and our stunning failures, our comic foibles and our tragic flaws. Throughout the world he is viewed as the most distinctively American of American authors — and as one of the most universal. He is assigned in classrooms in Naples, Riyadh, Belfast, and Beijing, and has been a major influence on twentieth-century writers from Argentina to Nigeria to Japan. The Oxford Mark Twain celebrates the versatility and vitality of this remarkable writer.

The Oxford Mark Twain reproduces the first American editions of Mark Twain's books published during his lifetime.[5] By encountering Twain's works in their original format — typography, layout, order of contents, and illustrations — readers today can come a few steps closer to the literary artifacts that entranced and excited readers when the books first appeared. Twain approved of and to a greater or lesser degree supervised the publication of all of this material.[6] The Mark Twain House in Hartford, Connecticut, generously loaned us its originals.[7] When more than one copy of a first American edition was available, Robert H. Hirst, general editor of the Mark Twain Project, in cooperation with Marianne Curling, curator of the Mark Twain House (and Jeffrey Kaimowitz, head of Rare Books for the Watkinson Library of Trinity College, Hartford, where the Mark Twain House collection is kept), guided our decision about which one to use.[8] As a set, the volumes also contain more than eighty essays commissioned especially for The Oxford Mark Twain, in which distinguished contributors reassess Twain's achievement as a writer and his place in the cultural conversation that he did so much to shape.

Each volume of The Oxford Mark Twain is introduced by a leading American, Canadian, or British writer who responds to Twain — often in a very personal way — as a fellow writer. Novelists, journalists, humorists, columnists, fabulists, poets, playwrights — these writers tell us what Twain taught them and what in his work continues to speak to them. Reading Twain's books, both famous and obscure, they reflect on the genesis of his art and the characteristics of his style, the themes he illuminated, and the aesthetic strategies he pioneered. Individually and collectively their contributions testify to the place Mark Twain holds in the hearts of readers of all kinds and temperaments.

Scholars whose work has shaped our view of Twain in the academy today have written afterwords to each volume, with suggestions for further reading. Their essays give us a sense of what was going on in Twain's life when he wrote the book at hand, and of how that book fits into his career. They explore how each book reflects and refracts contemporary events, and they show Twain responding to literary and social currents of the day, variously accepting, amplifying, modifying, and challenging prevailing paradigms. Sometimes they argue that works previously dismissed as quirky or eccentric departures actually address themes at the heart of Twain's work from the start. And as they bring new perspectives to Twain's composition strategies in familiar texts, several scholars see experiments in form where others saw only formlessness, method where prior critics saw only madness. In addition to elucidating the work's historical and cultural context, the afterwords provide an overview of responses to each book from its first appearance to the present.

Most of Mark Twain's books involved more than Mark Twain's words: unique illustrations. The parodic visual send-ups of "high culture" that Twain himself drew for *A Tramp Abroad*, the sketch of financial manipulator Jay Gould as a greedy and sadistic "Slave Driver" in *A Connecticut Yankee in King Arthur's Court*, and the memorable drawings of Eve in *Eve's Diary* all helped Twain's books to be sold, read, discussed, and preserved. In their essays for each volume that contains artwork, Beverly R. David and Ray Sapirstein highlight the significance of the sketches, engravings, and photographs in the first American editions of Mark Twain's works, and tell us what is known about the public response to them.

The Oxford Mark Twain invites us to read some relatively neglected works by Twain in the company of some of the most engaging literary figures of our time. Roy Blount Jr., for example, riffs in a deliciously Twain-like manner on "An Item Which the Editor Himself Could Not Understand," which may well rank as one of the least-known pieces Twain ever published. Bobbie Ann Mason celebrates the "mad energy" of Twain's most obscure comic novel, *The American Claimant*, in which the humor "hurtles beyond tall tale into simon-pure absurdity."[9] Garry Wills finds that *Christian Science* "gets us very close to the heart of American culture." Lee Smith reads "Political Economy" as a sharp and funny essay on language. Walter Mosley sees "The Stolen White Elephant," a story "reduced to a series of ridiculous telegrams related by an untrustworthy narrator caught up in an adventure that is as impossible as it is ludicrous," as a stunningly compact and economical satire of a world we still recognize as our own. Anne Bernays returns to "The Private History of a Campaign That Failed" and finds "an antiwar manifesto that is also confession, dramatic monologue, a plea for understanding and absolution, and a romp that gradually turns into atrocity even as we watch." After revisiting Captain Stormfield's heaven, Frederik Pohl finds that there "is no imaginable place more pleasant to spend eternity." Indeed, Pohl writes, "one would almost be willing to die to enter it."

While less familiar works receive fresh attention in The Oxford Mark Twain, new light is cast on the best-known works as well. Judith Martin ("Miss Manners") points out that it is by reading a court etiquette book that Twain's pauper learns how to behave as a proper prince. As important as etiquette may be in the palace, Martin notes, it is even more important in the slums.

> That etiquette is a sorer point with the ruffians in the street than with the proud dignitaries of the prince's court may surprise some readers. As in our own streets, etiquette is always a more volatile subject among those who cannot count on being treated with respect than among those who have the power to command deference.

And taking a fresh look at *Adventures of Huckleberry Finn*, Toni Morrison writes,

> much of the novel's genius lies in its quiescence, the silences that pervade it and give it a porous quality that is by turns brooding and soothing. It lies in . . . the subdued images in which the repetition of a simple word, such as "lonesome," tolls like an evening bell; the moments when nothing is said, when scenes and incidents swell the heart unbearably precisely because unarticulated, and force an act of imagination almost against the will.

Engaging Mark Twain as one writer to another, several contributors to The Oxford Mark Twain offer new insights into the processes by which his books came to be. Russell Banks, for example, reads *A Tramp Abroad* as "an important revision of Twain's incomplete first draft of *Huckleberry Finn*, a second draft, if you will, which in turn made possible the third and final draft." Erica Jong suggests that *1601*, a freewheeling parody of Elizabethan manners and mores, written during the same summer Twain began *Huckleberry Finn*, served as "a warm-up for his creative process" and "primed the pump for other sorts of freedom of expression." And Justin Kaplan suggests that "one of the transcendent figures standing behind and shaping" *Joan of Arc* was Ulysses S. Grant, whose memoirs Twain had recently published, and who, like Joan, had risen unpredictably "from humble and obscure origins" to become a "military genius" endowed with "the gift of command, a natural eloquence, and an equally natural reserve."

As a number of contributors note, Twain was a man ahead of his times. *The Gilded Age* was the first "Washington novel," Ward Just tells us, because "Twain was the first to see the possibilities that had eluded so many others." Commenting on *The Tragedy of Pudd'nhead Wilson*, Sherley Anne Williams observes that "Twain's argument about the power of environment in shaping character runs directly counter to prevailing sentiment where the negro was concerned." Twain's fictional technology, wildly fanciful by the standards of his day, predicts developments we take for granted in ours. DNA cloning, fax machines, and photocopiers are all prefigured, Bobbie Ann Mason tells us, in *The American Claimant*. Cynthia Ozick points out that the "telelectrophonoscope" we meet in "From the 'London Times' of 1904" is suspiciously like what we know as "television." And Malcolm Bradbury suggests that in the "phrenophones" of "Mental Telegraphy" "the Internet was born."

Twain turns out to have been remarkably prescient about political affairs as well. Kurt Vonnegut sees in *A Connecticut Yankee* a chilling foreshadowing (or perhaps a projection from the Civil War) of "all the high-tech atrocities which followed, and which follow still." Cynthia Ozick suggests that "The Man That Corrupted Hadleyburg," along with some of the other pieces collected under that title — many of them written when Twain lived in a Vienna ruled by Karl Lueger, a demagogue Adolf Hitler would later idolize — shoot up moral flares that shed an eerie light on the insidious corruption, prejudice, and hatred that reached bitter fruition under the Third Reich. And Twain's portrait in this book of "the dissolving Austria-Hungary of the 1890s," in Ozick's view, presages not only the Sarajevo that would erupt in 1914 but also "the disintegrated components of the former Yugoslavia" and "the *fin-de-siècle* Sarajevo of our own moment."

Despite their admiration for Twain's ambitious reach and scope, contributors to The Oxford Mark Twain also recognize his limitations. Mordecai Richler, for example, thinks that "the early pages of *Innocents Abroad* suffer from being a tad broad, proffering more burlesque than inspired satire," perhaps because Twain was "trying too hard for knee-slappers." Charles Johnson notes that the Young Man in Twain's philosophical dialogue about free will and determinism (*What Is Man?*) "caves in far too soon," failing to challenge what through late-twentieth-century eyes looks like "pseudoscience" and suspect essentialism in the Old Man's arguments.

Some contributors revisit their first encounters with Twain's works, recalling what surprised or intrigued them. When David Bradley came across "Fenimore Cooper's Literary Offences" in his college library, he "did not at first realize that Twain was being his usual ironic self with all this business about the 'nineteen rules governing literary art in the domain of romantic fiction,' but by the time I figured out there was no such list outside Twain's own head, I had decided that the rules made *sense*. . . . It seemed to me they were a pretty good blueprint for writing — Negro writing included." Sherley Anne Williams remembers that part of what attracted her to *Pudd'nhead Wilson* when she first read it thirty years ago was "that Twain, writing at the end of the nineteenth century, could imagine negroes as characters, albeit white ones, who actually thought for and of themselves, whose actions were the product of their thinking rather than the spontaneous ephemera of physical instincts that stereotype assigned to blacks." Frederik Pohl recalls his first reading of *Huckleberry Finn* as "a watershed event" in his life, the first book he read as a child in which "bad people" ceased to exercise a monopoly on doing "bad things." In *Huckleberry Finn* "some seriously bad things — things like the possession and mistreatment of black slaves, like stealing and lying, even like killing other people in duels — were quite often done by people who not only thought of themselves as exemplarily moral but, by any other standards I knew how to apply, actually *were* admirable citizens." The world that

Tom and Huck lived in, Pohl writes, "was filled with complexities and contradictions," and resembled "the world I appeared to be living in myself."

Other contributors explore their more recent encounters with Twain, explaining why they have revised their initial responses to his work. For Toni Morrison, parts of *Huckleberry Finn* that she "once took to be deliberate evasions, stumbles even, or a writer's impatience with his or her material," now strike her "as otherwise: as entrances, crevices, gaps, seductive invitations flashing the possibility of meaning. Unarticulated eddies that encourage diving into the novel's undertow — the real place where writer captures reader." One such "eddy" is the imprisonment of Jim on the Phelps farm. Instead of dismissing this portion of the book as authorial bungling, as she once did, Morrison now reads it as Twain's commentary on the 1880s, a period that "saw the collapse of civil rights for blacks," a time when "the nation, as well as Tom Sawyer, was deferring Jim's freedom in agonizing play." Morrison believes that Americans in the 1880s were attempting "to bury the combustible issues Twain raised in his novel," and that those who try to kick Huck Finn out of school in the 1990s are doing the same: "The cyclical attempts to remove the novel from classrooms extend Jim's captivity on into each generation of readers."

Although imitation-Hemingway and imitation-Faulkner writing contests draw hundreds of entries annually, no one has ever tried to mount a faux-Twain competition. Why? Perhaps because Mark Twain's voice is too much a part of who we are and how we speak even today. Roy Blount Jr. suggests that it is impossible, "at least for an American writer, to parody Mark Twain. It would be like doing an impression of your father or mother: he or she is already there in your voice."

Twain's style is examined and celebrated in The Oxford Mark Twain by fellow writers who themselves have struggled with the nuances of words, the structure of sentences, the subtleties of point of view, and the trickiness of opening lines. Bobbie Ann Mason observes, for example, that "Twain loved the sound of words and he knew how to string them by sound, like different shades of one color: 'The earl's barbaric eye,' 'the Usurping Earl,' 'a double-dyed humbug.'" Twain "relied on the punch of plain words" to show writers how to move beyond the "wordy romantic rubbish" so prevalent in nineteenth-century fiction, Mason says; he "was one of the first writers in America to deflower literary language." Lee Smith believes that "American writers have benefited as much from the way Mark Twain opened up the possibilities of first-person narration as we have from his use of vernacular language." (She feels that "the ghost of Mark Twain was hovering someplace in the background" when she decided to write her novel *Oral History* from the standpoint of multiple first-person narrators.) Frederick Busch maintains that "A Dog's Tale" "boasts one of the great opening sentences" of all time: "My father was a St. Bernard, my mother was a collie, but I am a Presbyterian." And Ursula Le Guin marvels at the ingenuity of the following sentence that she encounters in *Extracts from Adam's Diary.*

. . . This made her sorry for the creatures which live in there, which she calls fish, for she continues to fasten names on to things that don't need them and don't come when they are called by them, which is a matter of no consequence to her, as she is such a numskull anyway; so she got a lot of them out and brought them in last night and put them in my bed to keep warm, but I have noticed them now and then all day, and I don't see that they are any happier there than they were before, only quieter.[10]

Le Guin responds,

Now, that is a pure Mark-Twain-tour-de-force sentence, covering an immense amount of territory in an effortless, aimless ramble that seems to be heading nowhere in particular and ends up with breathtaking accuracy at the gold mine. Any sensible child would find that funny, perhaps not following all its divagations but delighted by the swing of it, by the word "numskull," by the idea of putting fish in the bed; and as that child grew older and reread it, its reward would only grow; and if that grown-up child had to write an essay on the piece and therefore earnestly studied and pored over this sentence, she would end up in unmitigated admiration of its vocabulary, syntax, pacing, sense, and rhythm, above all the beautiful timing of the last two words; and she would, and she does, still find it funny.

The fish surface again in a passage that Gore Vidal calls to our attention, from *Following the Equator*: "'The Whites always mean well when they take human fish out of the ocean and try to make them dry and warm and happy and comfortable in a chicken coop,' which is how, through civilization, they did away with many of the original inhabitants. Lack of empathy is a principal theme in Twain's meditations on race and empire."

Indeed, empathy — and its lack — is a principal theme in virtually all of Twain's work, as contributors frequently note. Nat Hentoff quotes the following thoughts from Huck in *Tom Sawyer Abroad*:

> I see a bird setting on a dead limb of a high tree, singing with its head tilted back and its mouth open, and before I thought I fired, and his song stopped and he fell straight down from the limb, all limp like a rag, and I run and picked him up and he was dead, and his body was warm in my hand, and his head rolled about this way and that, like his neck was broke, and there was a little white skin over his eyes, and one little drop of blood on the side of his head; and laws! I could n't see nothing more for the tears; and I hain't never murdered no creature since that war n't doing me no harm, and I ain't going to.[11]

"The Humane Society," Hentoff writes, "has yet to say anything as powerful — and lasting."

Readers of The Oxford Mark Twain will have the pleasure of revisiting Twain's Mississippi landmarks alongside Willie Morris, whose own lower Mississippi Valley boyhood gives him a special sense of connection to Twain. Morris knows firsthand the mosquitoes described in *Life on the Mississippi* — so colossal that "two of them could whip a dog" and "four of them could hold a man down"; in Morris's own hometown they were so large during the flood season that "local wags said they wore wristwatches." Morris's Yazoo City and Twain's Hannibal shared a "rough-hewn democracy . . . complicated by all the visible textures of caste and class, . . . harmless boyhood fun and mischief right along with . . . rank hypocrisies, churchgoing sanctimonies, racial hatred, entrenched and unrepentant greed."

For the West of Mark Twain's *Roughing It*, readers will have George Plimpton as their guide. "What a group these newspapermen were!" Plimpton writes about Twain and his friends Dan De Quille and Joe Goodman in Virginia City, Nevada. "Their roisterous carryings-on bring to mind the kind of frat-house enthusiasm one associates with college humor magazines like the *Harvard Lampoon*." Malcolm Bradbury examines Twain as "a living example of what made the American so different from the European." And Hal Holbrook, who has interpreted Mark Twain on stage for some forty years, describes how Twain "played" during the civil rights movement, during the Vietnam War, during the Gulf War, and in Prague on the eve of the demise of Communism.

Why do we continue to read Mark Twain? What draws us to him? His wit? His compassion? His humor? His bravura? His humility? His understanding of who and what we are in those parts of our being that we rarely open to view? Our sense that he knows we can do better than we do? Our sense that he knows we can't? E. L. Doctorow tells us that children are attracted to *Tom Sawyer* because in this book "the young reader confirms his own hope that no matter how troubled his relations with his elders may be, beneath all their disapproval is their underlying love for him, constant and steadfast." Readers in general, Arthur Miller writes, value Twain's "insights into America's always uncertain moral life and its shifting but everlasting hypocrisies"; we appreciate the fact that he "is not using his alienation from the public illusions of his hour in order to reject the country implicitly as though he could live without it, but manifestly in order to correct it." Perhaps we keep reading Mark Twain because, in Miller's words, he "wrote much more like a father than a son. He doesn't seem to be sitting in class taunting the teacher but standing at the head of it challenging his students to acknowledge their own humanity, that is, their immemorial attraction to the untrue."

Mark Twain entered the public eye at a time when many of his countrymen considered "American culture" an oxymoron; he died four years before a world conflagration that would lead many to question whether the contradiction in terms was not "European civilization" instead. In between he worked in journalism, printing, steamboating, mining, lecturing, publishing, and editing, in virtually every region of the country. He tried his hand at humorous sketches, social satire, historical novels, children's books, poetry, drama, science fiction, mysteries, romance, philosophy, travelogue, memoir, polemic, and several genres no one had ever seen before or has ever seen since. He invented a self-pasting scrapbook, a history game, a vest strap, and a gizmo for keeping bed sheets tucked in; he invested in machines and processes designed to revolutionize typesetting and engraving, and in a food supplement called "Plasmon." Along the way he cheerfully impersonated himself and prior versions of himself for doting publics on five continents while playing out a charming rags-to-riches story followed by a devastating riches-to-rags story followed by yet another great American comeback. He had a long-running real-life engagement in a sumptuous comedy of manners, and then in a real-life tragedy not of his own design: during the last fourteen years of his life almost everyone he ever loved was taken from him by disease and death.

Mark Twain has indelibly shaped our views of who and what the United States is as a nation and of who and what we might become. He understood the nostalgia for a "simpler" past that increased as that past receded — and he saw through the nostalgia to a past that was just as complex as the present. He recognized better than we did ourselves our potential for greatness and our potential for disaster. His fictions brilliantly illuminated the world in which he lived, changing it — and us — in the process. He knew that our feet often danced to tunes that had somehow remained beyond our hearing; with perfect pitch he played them back to us.

My mother read *Tom Sawyer* to me as a bedtime story when I was eleven. I thought Huck and Tom could be a lot of fun, but I dismissed Becky Thatcher as a bore. When I was twelve I invested a nickel at a local garage sale in a book that contained short pieces by Mark Twain. That was where I met Twain's Eve. Now, *that's* more like it, I decided, pleased to meet a female character I could identify *with* instead of against. Eve had spunk. Even if she got a lot wrong, you had to give her credit for trying. "The Man That Corrupted

Hadleyburg" left me giddy with satisfaction: none of my adolescent reveries of getting even with my enemies were half as neat as the plot of the man who got back at that town. "How I Edited an Agricultural Paper" set me off in uncontrollable giggles.

People sometimes told me that I looked like Huck Finn. "It's the freckles," they'd explain — not explaining anything at all. I didn't read *Huckleberry Finn* until junior year in high school in my English class. It was the fall of 1965. I was living in a small town in Connecticut. I expected a sequel to *Tom Sawyer*. So when the teacher handed out the books and announced our assignment, my jaw dropped: "Write a paper on how Mark Twain used irony to attack racism in *Huckleberry Finn*."

The year before, the bodies of three young men who had gone to Mississippi to help blacks register to vote — James Chaney, Andrew Goodman, and Michael Schwerner — had been found in a shallow grave; a group of white segregationists (the county sheriff among them) had been arrested in connection with the murders. America's inner cities were simmering with pent-up rage that began to explode in the summer of 1965, when riots in Watts left thirty-four people dead. None of this made any sense to me. I was confused, angry, certain that there was something missing from the news stories I read each day: the why. Then I met Pap Finn. And the Phelpses.

Pap Finn, Huck tells us, "had been drunk over in town" and "was just all mud." He erupts into a drunken tirade about "a free nigger . . . from Ohio — a mulatter, most as white as a white man," with "the whitest shirt on you ever see, too, and the shiniest hat; and there ain't a man in town that's got as fine clothes as what he had."

> . . . they said he was a p'fessor in a college, and could talk all kinds of languages, and knowed everything. And that ain't the wust. They said he could *vote*, when he was at home. Well, that let me out. Thinks I, what is the country a-coming to? It was 'lection day, and I was just about to go and vote, myself, if I warn't too drunk to get there; but when they told me there was a State in this country where they'd let that nigger vote, I drawed out. I says I'll never vote agin. Them's the very words I said. . . . And to see the

cool way of that nigger — why, he wouldn't a give me the road if I hadn't
shoved him out o' the way.[12]

Later on in the novel, when the runaway slave Jim gives up his freedom to
nurse a wounded Tom Sawyer, a white doctor testifies to the stunning altru-
ism of his actions. The Phelpses and their neighbors, all fine, upstanding,
well-meaning, churchgoing folk,

agreed that Jim had acted very well, and was deserving to have some notice
took of it, and reward. So every one of them promised, right out and
hearty, that they wouldn't curse him no more.

Then they come out and locked him up. I hoped they was going to say
he could have one or two of the chains took off, because they was rotten
heavy, or could have meat and greens with his bread and water, but they
didn't think of it.[13]

Why did the behavior of these people tell me more about why Watts
burned than anything I had read in the daily paper? And why did a drunk
Pap Finn railing against a black college professor from Ohio whose vote was
as good as his own tell me more about white anxiety over black political
power than anything I had seen on the evening news?

Mark Twain knew that there was nothing, absolutely *nothing*, a black man
could do — including selflessly sacrificing his freedom, the only thing of value
he had — that would make white society see beyond the color of his skin. And
Mark Twain knew that depicting racists with chilling accuracy would expose
the viciousness of their world view like nothing else could. It was an insight
echoed some eighty years after Mark Twain penned Pap Finn's rantings
about the black professor, when Malcolm X famously asked, "Do you know
what white racists call black Ph.D.'s?" and answered, "'*Nigger!*'"[14]

Mark Twain taught me things I needed to know. He taught me to understand the raw racism that lay behind what I saw on the evening news. He
taught me that the most well-meaning people can be hurtful and myopic. He
taught me to recognize the supreme irony of a country founded in freedom
that continued to deny freedom to so many of its citizens. Every time I hear of

another effort to kick Huck Finn out of school somewhere, I recall everything that Mark Twain taught *this* high school junior, and I find myself jumping into the fray.[15] I remember the black high school student who called CNN during the phone-in portion of a 1985 debate between Dr. John Wallace, a black educator spearheading efforts to ban the book, and myself. She accused Dr. Wallace of insulting her and all black high school students by suggesting they weren't smart enough to understand Mark Twain's irony. And I recall the black cameraman on the *CBS Morning News* who came up to me after he finished shooting another debate between Dr. Wallace and myself. He said he had never read the book by Mark Twain that we had been arguing about — but now he really wanted to. One thing that puzzled him, though, was why a white woman was defending it and a black man was attacking it, because as far as he could see from what we'd been saying, the book made whites look pretty bad.

As I came to understand *Huckleberry Finn* and *Pudd'nhead Wilson* as commentaries on the era now known as the nadir of American race relations, those books pointed me toward the world recorded in nineteenth-century black newspapers and periodicals and in fiction by Mark Twain's black contemporaries. My investigation of the role black voices and traditions played in shaping Mark Twain's art helped make me aware of their role in shaping all of American culture.[16] My research underlined for me the importance of changing the stories we tell about who we are to reflect the realities of what we've been.[17]

Ever since our encounter in high school English, Mark Twain has shown me the potential of American literature and American history to illuminate each other. Rarely have I found a contradiction or complexity we grapple with as a nation that Mark Twain had not puzzled over as well. He insisted on taking America seriously. And he insisted on *not* taking America seriously: "I think that there is but a single specialty with us, only one thing that can be called by the wide name 'American,'" he once wrote. "That is the national devotion to ice-water."[18]

Mark Twain threw back at us our dreams and our denial of those dreams, our greed, our goodness, our ambition, and our laziness, all rattling around together in that vast echo chamber of our talk — that sharp, spunky American talk that Mark Twain figured out how to write down without robbing it of its energy and immediacy. Talk shaped by voices that the official arbiters of "culture" deemed of no importance — voices of children, voices of slaves, voices of servants, voices of ordinary people. Mark Twain listened. And he made us listen. To the stories he told us, and to the truths they conveyed. He still has a lot to say that we need to hear.

Mark Twain lives — in our libraries, classrooms, homes, theaters, movie houses, streets, and most of all in our speech. His optimism energizes us, his despair sobers us, and his willingness to keep wrestling with the hilarious and horrendous complexities of it all keeps us coming back for more. As the twenty-first century approaches, may he continue to goad us, chasten us, delight us, berate us, and cause us to erupt in unrestrained laughter in unexpected places.

NOTES

1. Ernest Hemingway, *Green Hills of Africa* (New York: Charles Scribner's Sons, 1935), 22. George Bernard Shaw to Samuel L. Clemens, July 3, 1907, quoted in Albert Bigelow Paine, *Mark Twain: A Biography* (New York: Harper and Brothers, 1912), 3:1398.

2. Allen Carey-Webb, "Racism and *Huckleberry Finn*: Censorship, Dialogue and Change," *English Journal* 82, no. 7 (November 1993):22.

3. See Louis J. Budd, "Impersonators," in J. R. LeMaster and James D. Wilson, eds., *The Mark Twain Encyclopedia* (New York: Garland Publishing Company, 1993), 389–91.

4. See Shelley Fisher Fishkin, "Ripples and Reverberations," part 3 of *Lighting Out for the Territory: Reflections on Mark Twain and American Culture* (New York: Oxford University Press, 1996).

5. There are two exceptions. Twain published chapters from his autobiography in the *North American Review* in 1906 and 1907, but this material was not published in book form in Twain's lifetime; our volume reproduces the material as it appeared in the *North American Review*. The other exception is our final volume, *Mark Twain's Speeches*, which appeared two months after Twain's death in 1910.

An unauthorized handful of copies of *1601* was privately printed by an Alexander Gunn of Cleveland at the instigation of Twain's friend John Hay in 1880. The first American edition authorized by Mark Twain, however, was printed at the United States Military Academy at West Point in 1882; that is the edition reproduced here.

It should further be noted that four volumes — *The Stolen White Elephant and Other Detective Stories, Following the Equator and Anti-imperialist Essays, The Diaries of Adam and Eve,* and *1601, and Is Shakespeare Dead?* — bind together material originally published separately. In each case the first American edition of the material is the version that has been reproduced, always in its entirety. Because Twain constantly recycled and repackaged previously published works in his collections of short pieces, a certain amount of duplication is unavoidable. We have selected volumes with an eye toward keeping this duplication to a minimum.

Even the twenty-nine-volume Oxford Mark Twain has had to leave much out. No edition of Twain can ever claim to be "complete," for the man was too prolix, and the file drawers of both ephemera and as yet unpublished texts are deep.

6. With the possible exception of *Mark Twain's Speeches.* Some scholars suspect Twain knew about this book and may have helped shape it, although no hard evidence to that effect has yet surfaced. Twain's involvement in the production process varied greatly from book to book. For a fuller sense of authorial intention, scholars will continue to rely on the superb definitive editions of Twain's works produced by the Mark Twain Project at the University of California at Berkeley as they become available. Dense with annotation documenting textual emendation and related issues, these editions add immeasurably to our understanding of Mark Twain and the genesis of his works.

7. Except for a few titles that were not in its collection. The American Antiquarian Society in Worcester, Massachusetts, provided the first edition of *King Leopold's Soliloquy;* the Elmer Holmes Bobst Library of New York University furnished the 1906–7 volumes of the *North American Review* in which *Chapters from My Autobiography* first appeared; the Harry Ransom Humanities Research Center at the University of Texas at Austin made their copy of the West Point edition of *1601* available; and the Mark Twain Project provided the first edition of *Extract from Captain Stormfield's Visit to Heaven.*

8. The specific copy photographed for Oxford's facsimile edition is indicated in a note on the text at the end of each volume.

9. All quotations from contemporary writers in this essay are taken from their introductions to the volumes of The Oxford Mark Twain, and the quotations from Mark Twain's works are taken from the texts reproduced in The Oxford Mark Twain.

10. *The Diaries of Adam and Eve,* The Oxford Mark Twain [hereafter OMT] (New York: Oxford University Press, 1996), p. 33.

11. *Tom Sawyer Abroad,* OMT, p. 74.

12. *Adventures of Huckleberry Finn,* OMT, p. 49–50.

13. Ibid., p. 358.

14. Malcolm X, *The Autobiography of Malcolm X,* with the assistance of Alex Haley (New York: Grove Press, 1965), p. 284.

15. I do not mean to minimize the challenge of teaching this difficult novel, a challenge for which all teachers may not feel themselves prepared. Elsewhere I have developed some concrete strategies for approaching the book in the classroom, including teaching it in the context of the history of American race relations and alongside books by black writers. See Shelley Fisher Fishkin, "Teaching *Huckleberry Finn*," in James S. Leonard, ed., *Making Mark Twain Work in the Classroom* (Durham: Duke University Press, forthcoming). See also Shelley Fisher Fishkin, *Was Huck Black? Mark Twain and African-American Voices* (New York: Oxford University Press, 1993), pp. 106–8, and a curriculum kit in preparation at the Mark Twain House in Hartford, containing teaching suggestions from myself, David Bradley, Jocelyn Chadwick-Joshua, James Miller, and David E. E. Sloane.

16. See Fishkin, *Was Huck Black?* See also Fishkin, "Interrogating 'Whiteness,' Complicating 'Blackness': Remapping American Culture," in Henry Wonham, ed., *Criticism and the Color Line: Desegregating American Literary Studies* (New Brunswick: Rutgers UP, 1996, pp. 251–90 and in shortened form in *American Quarterly* 47, no. 3 (September 1995):428–66.

17. I explore the roots of my interest in Mark Twain and race at greater length in an essay entitled "Changing the Story," in Jeffrey Rubin-Dorsky and Shelley Fisher Fishkin, eds., *People of the Book: Thirty Scholars Reflect on Their Jewish Identity* (Madison: U of Wisconsin Press, 1996), pp. 47–63.

18. "What Paul Bourget Thinks of Us," *How to Tell a Story and Other Essays*, OMT, p. 197.

INTRODUCTION
Reading Young, Reading Old
Ursula K. Le Guin

Every tribe has its myths, and the younger members of the tribe generally get them wrong. My tribal myth of the great Berkeley Fire of 1923 went this way: when my mother's mother-in-law, who lived near the top of Cedar Street, saw the flames sweeping over the hill straight towards the house, she put her Complete Works of Mark Twain in Twenty-five Volumes into her Model A and went away from that place.

Because I was going to put that story in print, I made the mistake of checking it first with my brother Ted. In a slow, mild sort of way, he took it all to pieces. He said, Well, Lena Brown never had a Model A. As a matter of fact, she didn't drive. The way I remember the story, he said, some fraternity boys came up the street and got her piano out just before the fire reached that hill. And a bearskin rug, and some other things. But I don't remember, he said, that anything was said about the Complete Works of Mark Twain.

He and I agreed, however, that fraternity boys who would choose to rescue a piano and a bear rug from a house about to be engulfed by a fiery inferno might well have also selected the works of Mark Twain. And the peculiarity of their selection may be illuminated by the fact that the piano ended up in the fraternity house. But after the fire or during it, Lena Brown somehow rescued the bear rug and the Complete Works from her rescuers; because Ted remembers the bear; and I certainly, vividly remember the Complete Works.

I also remain convinced that she was very fond of them, that she *would* have rescued them rather than her clothes and silver and checkbook. And maybe she really did. At any rate, when she died she left them to the family, and my brothers and I grew up with them, a full shelf of lightweight, middle-sized books in slightly pebbly and rather ratty red bindings. They are no longer, alas, in the family, but I have tracked down the edition in a library. As soon as I saw the row of red books I said Yes! with the startled joy one would feel at seeing an adult one had loved as a child, alive and looking just as he did fifty years ago. Our set was, to the best of my knowledge, the 1917 Authorized Uniform Edition, published by Harper and Brothers, copyright by the Mark Twain Company.

The only other Complete Works I recall around the house was my Great-Aunt Betsy's Dickens. I was proud of both sets. Complete Works and Uniform Editions are something you don't often see any more except in big libraries, but ordinary people used to own them and be proud of them. They have a majesty about them. Physically they are imposing, the uniform row of bindings, the gold-stamped titles; but the true majesty of a Complete Works is spiritual. It is a great mental edifice, a house of many mansions, into which a reader can enter at any of the doors, or a young reader can climb in the windows, and wander about, experiencing magnanimity.

My great-aunt was very firm about not letting us get into Dickens yet. She said nobody under eighteen had any business reading Dickens. We would merely misunderstand him and so spoil the pleasure we would otherwise take in him the rest of our lives. She was right, and I am grateful. At sixteen, I whined till she let me read *David Copperfield*, but she warned me about Steerforth, lest I fall in love with him as she had done, and break my heart. When Betsy died she left me her Dickens. We had him re-bound, for he had got a bit shabby traveling around the West with her for fifty or sixty years. When I take a book from that set, I think how she had this immense refuge and resource with her wherever she went, reliable as not much else in her life was.

Except for Dickens, nobody told us not to read anything, and I burrowed headlong into every book on the shelves. If it was a story, I read it. And there stood that whole row of red books, all full of stories.

Obviously I got to *Tom Sawyer* very soon, and *Huckleberry Finn*; and my next-older brother, Karl, showed me the sequels, which we judged pretty inferior, critical brats that we were. After *The Prince and the Pauper*, I got into *Life on the Mississippi* and *Roughing It* — my prime favorite for years — and the stories, and the whole Complete Works in fact, one red book after the other, snap, munch, gulp, snap, munch, gulp.

I didn't much like the Connecticut Yankee. The meaning of the book went right over my head. I just thought the hero was a pigheaded, loudmouthed show-off. But a little thing like not *liking* a book didn't keep me from *reading* it. Not then. It was like Brussels sprouts. Nobody could like them, but they existed, they were food, you ate them. Eating and reading were a central, essential part of life. Eating and reading can't all be Huck and corn on the cob; some of it has to be Brussels sprouts and the Yankee. And there were plenty of good bits in the Yankee. The only one of the row of red books I ever stuck at was *Joan of Arc*. I just couldn't swallow her. She wouldn't go down. And I believe our set was lacking the *Christian Science* volume, because I don't remember even having a go at that. If it had been there, I would have chewed at it, the way kids do, the way Eskimo housewives soften walrus hide, though I might not have been able to swallow it either.

My memory is that it was Karl who discovered Adam's and Eve's diaries and told me to read them. I have always followed Karl's advice in reading, even after he became an English professor, because he never led me astray before he was a professor. I never would have got into *Tom Brown's School Days*, for instance, if he hadn't told me you can skip the first sixty pages, and it must have been Karl who told me to stick with *Candide* till I got to the person with one buttock, who would make it all worthwhile. So I found the right red book and read both the diaries. I loved them instantly and permanently.

And yet when I reread them not long ago, it was the first time for about fifty years. Not having the Complete Works with me throughout life, I have only reread my favorites of the books, picked up here and there, and the stories contained in various collections. And none of those collections contained the diaries.

This five-decade gap in time makes it irresistible to try and compare my reading of the diaries as a child with my reading of them now.

The first thing to be said is that when I reread them, there did not seem to have been any gap at all. What's fifty years? Well, when it comes to some of the books one read at five or at fifteen, it's an abyss. Many books I loved and learned from have fallen into it. I absolutely cannot read *The Swiss Family Robinson* and am amazed that I ever did — talk about chewing walrus hide! But the diaries give me a curious feeling of constancy, almost of immortality: because *they* haven't changed at all. They are just as fresh and surprising as when I read them first. Nor am I sure that my reading of them is very different from what it was back then.

I will try to follow that then-and-now response through three aspects of the diaries, humor, gender, and religion.

Though it seems that children and adults have different senses of humor, they overlap so much I wonder if people just don't use the same apparatus differently at different ages. At about the time I first came on the diaries, ten or eleven, I was reading the stories of James Thurber with sober, pious attention. I knew they were funny, that grown-ups laughed aloud reading them, but they didn't make me laugh. They were wonderful, mysterious tales of human behavior, like all the folktales and stories in which people did the amazing, terrifying, inexplicable things that grown-ups do. The various night wanderings of the Thurber family in "The Night the Bed Fell Down" were no more and no less strange to me than the behavior of the Reed family in the first chapter of *Jane Eyre*. Both were fascinating descriptions of life — eyewitness accounts, guidebooks to the world awaiting me. I was much too interested to laugh.

When I did laugh at Thurber was when he played with words. The man who came with the reeves and the cook who was alarmed by the dome-shaped thing on top of the refrigerator were a source of pure delight to me, then as now. The accessibility of Mark Twain's humor to a child surely has much to do with the way he plays with language, the deadpan absurdities, the marvelous choices of word. The first time I read the story about the bluejay trying to fill the cabin with acorns, I nearly died. I lay on the floor gasping and writhing with joy. Even now I feel a peaceful cheer come over me when I think of that bluejay. And it's all in the way he tells it, as they say. The story is the way the story is told.

Adam's diary is funny, when it is funny, because of the way Adam writes it.

... This made her sorry for the creatures which live in there, which she calls fish, for she continues to fasten names on to things that don't need them and don't come when they are called by them, which is a matter of no consequence to her, as she is such a numskull anyway; so she got a lot of them out and brought them in last night and put them in my bed to keep warm, but I have noticed them now and then all day, and I don't see that they are any happier there than they were before, only quieter.

Now that is a pure Mark-Twain-tour-de-force sentence, covering an immense amount of territory in an effortless, aimless ramble that seems to be heading nowhere in particular and ends up with breathtaking accuracy at the gold mine. Any sensible child would find that funny, perhaps not following all its divagations but delighted by the swing of it, by the word "numskull," by the idea of putting fish in the bed; and as that child grew older and reread it, its reward would only grow; and if that grown-up child had to write an essay on the piece and therefore earnestly studied and pored over this sentence, she would end up in unmitigated admiration of its vocabulary, syntax, pacing, sense, and rhythm, above all the beautiful timing of the last two words; and she would, and she does, still find it funny.

Twain's humor is indestructible. Trying to make a study of the rhythms of prose last year, I analyzed a paragraph from the jumping frog story — laboring over it, dissecting it, counting beats, grouping phrases, reducing it to a mere drum score — and even after all that mauling, every time I read it, it was as fresh-flowing and lively and amusing as ever, or more so. The prose itself is indestructible. It is all of a piece. It is a living person speaking. Mark Twain put his voice on paper with a fidelity and vitality that makes electronic recordings seem crude and quaint.

I wonder if this is why we trust him, even though he lets us down so often. Lapses such as the silly stuff about Niagara in Adam's diary — evidently stuffed in to make it suit a publication about the Falls — would make me distrust most writers. But Mark Twain's purity is unmistakable and incorruptible, which is why the lapses stick out so, and yet are forgivable. I have heard a great pianist who made a great many mistakes in playing; the mistakes were of no account because the music was true. Though Mark Twain forces his humor sometimes, always his own voice comes back, comes through; and his own voice is one of hyperbole and absurdity and wild invention and absolute truth.

So all in all my response to the humor of the diaries is very much what it was fifty years ago. This is partly because a good deal of the humor is perfectly childish. I mean that as praise. There is no meanness in it, no nudging and winking, nothing snide. Now, as then, I find Adam very funny, but so obtuse I often want to kick him rather than laugh at him. Eve isn't quite as funny, but I don't get as cross with her, so it's easier to laugh.

A parenthesis. The illustrations which accompany the texts used for this edition pose a puzzle to me. The 1917 Authorized Edition in the library, "my" edition, does not contain any illustrations to Adam's diary at all; and yet Strothmann's "stone-carving" pictures were perfectly familiar. Where have I ever seen them before? I don't know. They certainly seem to belong. Yet — now — I am aware that they're not only amusing and inventive decorations, but also ironically interpret the text. For instance, on a Sunday when Adam's only diary entry is a sullen "Pulled through," the picture shows him in a Morris chair smoking a stogie and reading the papers in perfect Sunday luxury. Even as a child, I realized that Adam was what we now call an unreliable narrator. But it does appear that the illustrator went further than Mark Twain intended in betraying Adam's self-pity.

The 1917 edition contains only the first and the last of Lester Ralph's illustrations to Eve's diary, and no mention of the artist's name. I recognized those two with delight when I saw them again. I would have liked them all, as a child; their art nouveau style was familiar to me from picture books, and I felt at home with it. Though the whole set is rather repetitive, the pictures have charm and elegance; the line is sure and clean; and Eve is the robust and joyous young woman she ought to be. The text is, I think, genuinely enriched by them, though they bring out its sweetness rather than its humor.

I read the diaries before I had any personal interest, as you might say, in gender. I had noticed that there were males and females and had learned from a useful Germanic book how babies occurred, but the whole thing was entirely remote and theoretical, about as immediately interesting to me as the Keynesian theory of economics. "Latency," one of Freud's fine imaginative inventions, was more successful than most; children used to have years of freedom before they had to start working their hormones into the kind of lascivious lather that is now expected of ten-year-olds. Anyhow, in the 1940s gender was not a subject of discussion. Men were men (running things or in uniform, mostly), women were women (housekeeping or in factories, mostly), and that was that. Except for a few subversives like Virginia Woolf, nobody publicly questioned the institutions and assumptions of male primacy. It was the century's low point architecturally in the Construction of Gender, reduced in those years to something about as spacious and comfortable as a broom closet.

But the diaries date from the turn of the century, a time of revolutionary inquiry into gender roles, the first age of feminism, the period of the woman suffrage movement and of the "New Woman" — who was precisely the robust and joyously competent Eve that Mark Twain gives us.

I see now in the diaries, along with a tenderness and a profound delicacy of feeling about women, a certain advocacy. Mark Twain is always on the side of the underdog; and though he believed it was and must be a man's world, he knew that women were the underdogs in it. This fine sense of justice is what gives both the diaries their moral complexity.

There was an element of discomfort in them for me as a child, and I think it lies just here, in that complexity and a certain degree of self-contradiction.

It is not Adam's superiority of brains or brawn, but his blockish stupidity, that gives him his absolute advantage over Eve. He does not notice, does not

XXXVIII : URSULA K. LE GUIN

listen, is uninterested, indifferent, dumb. He will not relate to her; she must relate herself — in words and actions — to him, and relate him to the rest of Eden. He is entirely satisfied with himself as he is; she must adapt her ways to him. He is immovably fixed at the center of his own attention. To live with him she must agree to be peripheral to him, contingent, secondary.

The degree of social and psychological truth in this picture of life in Eden is pretty considerable. Milton thought it was a fine arrangement; it appears Mark Twain didn't, since he shows us at the end of both diaries that although Eve has not changed much, she has changed Adam profoundly. She always was awake. He slowly, finally wakes up, and does her, and therefore himself, justice. But isn't it too late, for her?

All this I think I followed pretty well, and was fascinated and somewhat troubled by, though I could not have discussed it, when I read the diaries as a child. Children have a seemingly innate passion for justice; they don't have to be taught it. They have to have it beaten out of them, in fact, to end up as properly prejudiced adults.

Mark Twain and I both grew up in a society that cherished a visionary ideal of gender by pairs: the breadwinning, self-reliant husband and the home-dwelling, dependent wife. He the oak, she the ivy; power his, grace hers. He works and earns; she "doesn't work," but she keeps his house, bears and brings up his children, and furnishes him the aesthetic and often the spiritual comforts of life. Now, at this latter end of the century, the religiopolitical conservative's vision of what men and women do and should do is still close to that picture, though even more remote from most people's experience than it was fifty or a hundred years ago. Do Twain's Adam and Eve essentially fit this powerful stereotype, or do they vary it significantly?

I think the variations are significant, even if the text fudges them in the end. Mark Twain is not supporting a gender ideal, but investigating what he sees as real differences between women and men, some of them fitting into that ideal, some in conflict with it.

Eve is the intellectual in Eden, Adam the redneck. She is wildly curious and wants to learn everything, to name everything. Adam has no curiosity about anything, certain that he knows all he needs to know. She wants to talk, he wants to grunt. She is sociable, he is solitary. She prides herself on being scientific, though she settles for her own pet theory without testing it; her method is purely intuitive and rational, without a shadow of empiricism. He thinks she ought to test her ideas, but is too lazy to do it himself. He goes over Niagara Falls in a barrel, he doesn't say why; apparently because a man does such things. Far more influenced by imagination than he, she does dangerous things only when she doesn't know they're dangerous. She rides tigers and talks to the serpent. She is rebellious, adventurous, and independent; he does not question authority. She is the innocent troublemaker. Her loving anarchism ruins his mindless, self-sufficient, authoritarian Eden — and saves him from it.

Does it save her?

This spirited, intelligent, anarchic Eve reminds me of H. G. Wells's Ann Veronica, an exemplary New Woman of 1909. Yet Ann Veronica's courage and curiosity finally lead her not to independence but to wifehood, seen as the proper and sufficient fulfillment of feminine being. We are ominously close to the Natasha Syndrome, the collapse of a vivid woman character into a brood sow as soon as she marries and has children. Once she has won Adam over, once the children come, does Eve stop asking and thinking and singing and naming and venturing? We don't know. Tolstoy gives us a horrible glimpse of Natasha married; Wells tries to convince us Ann Veronica is going to be just fine; but Mark Twain tells us nothing about what Eve becomes. She falls silent, which is not a good sign. After the Fall we have mostly Adam's voice, puzzling mightly over what kind of animal Cain is. Eve tells us only that she would love Adam even if he beat her — a very bad sign. And, forty years after, she says, "He is strong, I am weak, I am not so necessary to him as he is to me — life without him would not be life; how could I endure it?"

I don't know whether I am supposed to believe her, or can believe her. It doesn't sound like the woman I knew. Eve, weak? Rubbish! Adam's usefulness as a helpmeet is problematic: a man who, when she tells him they'll have to work for their living, decides, "She will be useful. I will superintend" — a

XL : URSULA K. LE GUIN

man who thinks his son is a kangaroo? Eve did need him in order to have children, and since she loves him she would miss him; but where is the evidence that she couldn't survive without him? He would presumably have survived without her, in the brutish way he survived before her. But surely it is their *interdependence* that is the real point?

I want, now, to read the diaries as a subtle, sweet-natured send-up of the Strong Man/Weak Woman arrangement; but I'm not sure it's possible to do so, or not entirely. It may be both a send-up and a capitulation.

And Adam has the last word. But the poignancy of those six last words is utterly unexpected, a cry from the heart. It made me shiver as a child; it does now.

I was raised as irreligious as a jackrabbit, and probably this is one reason Mark Twain made so much sense to me as a child. Descriptions of churchgoing interested me as the exotic rites of a foreign tribe, and nobody described churchgoing better than Mark Twain did. But God, as I encountered him in my reading, seemed only to cause unnecessary complications, making people fall into strange postures and do depressing things; he treated Beth March abominably, and did his best to ruin Jane Eyre's life before she traded him in for Rochester. I didn't read any of the books in which God is the main character until a few years later. I was perfectly content with books in which he didn't figure at all.

Could anybody but Mark Twain have told the story of Adam and Eve without mentioning Jehovah?

As a heathen child I was entirely comfortable with his version. I took it for granted that it was the sensible one.

As an ancient heathen I still find it sensible, but can better appreciate its orginality and courage. The nerve of the man, the marvelous, stunning independence of that mind! In pious, prayerful, censorious, self-righteous Christian America of 1896, or 1996 for that matter, to show God as an unnecessary hypothesis, by letting Eve and Adam cast themselves out of Eden without any help at all from him, and really none from the serpent either — to put sin and salvation, love and death, in our own hands, as our own, strictly human business, our responsibility — now that's a free soul, and a brave one.

What luck for a child to meet such a soul when she is young. What luck for a country to have a Mark Twain in its heart.

EXTRACTS FROM

ADAM'S DIARY

EXTRACTS FROM
ADAM'S DIARY
—
MARK TWAIN

WRITING HIS DIARY

Extracts From Adam's Diary

TRANSLATED FROM THE ORIGINAL MS.

By Mark Twain

ILLUSTRATED BY
F. STROTHMANN

NEW YORK AND LONDON
HARPER & BROTHERS
PUBLISHERS :: MCMIV

[NOTE.—*I translated a portion of this diary some years ago, and a friend of mine printed a few copies in an incomplete form, but the public never got them. Since then I have deciphered some more of Adam's hieroglyphics, and think he has now become sufficiently important as a public character to justify this publication.*—M. T.]

Extracts
From Adam's Diary

Translated from the original MS.

Extracts from Adam's Diary

Extracts From Adam's Diary

Translated from the original MS.

Monday

This new creature with the long
hair is a good deal in the way. It is
always hanging around and following
me about. I don't like this; I am not
used to company. I wish it would
stay with the other animals. . . .
Cloudy to-day, wind in the east; think
we shall have rain. . . . *We?* Where
did I get that word? . . . I remember
now—the new creature uses it.

4

Tuesday

Been examining the great waterfall. It is the finest thing on the estate, I think. The new creature calls it Niagara Falls—why, I am sure I do not know. Says it *looks* like Niagara Falls. That is not a reason; it is mere waywardness and imbecility. I get no chance to name anything myself. The new creature names everything that comes along, before I can get in a protest. And always that same pretext is offered—it *looks* like the thing. There is the dodo, for instance. Says the moment one looks at it one sees at a glance that it "looks like a dodo." It will have to keep that name, no doubt. It wearies me to fret about it, and it does no good, anyway. Dodo! It looks no more like a dodo than I do.

Wednesday

Built me a shelter against the rain, but could not have it to myself in peace. The new creature intruded. When I tried to put it out it shed water out of the holes it looks with, and wiped it away with the back of its paws, and made a noise such as some of the other animals make when they are in distress. I wish it would not talk; it is always talking. That sounds like a cheap fling at the poor creature, a slur; but I do not mean it so. I have never heard the human voice before, and any new and strange sound intruding itself here upon the solemn hush of these dreaming solitudes offends my ear and seems a false note. And this new sound is so close to me; it is right at my shoulder, right at my ear, first on one side and

Wednesday

then on the other, and I am used only
to sounds that are more or less dis-
tant from me.

Friday

The naming goes recklessly on, in spite of anything I can do. I had a very good name for the estate, and it was musical and pretty—GARDEN-OF-EDEN. Privately, I continue to call it that, but not any longer publicly. The new creature says it is all woods and rocks and scenery, and therefore has no resemblance to a garden. Says it *looks* like a park, and does not look like anything *but* a park. Consequently, without consulting me, it has been new-named —NIAGARA FALLS PARK. This is sufficiently high-handed, it seems to me. And already there is a sign up:

```
KEEP OFF
THE GRASS
```

My life is not as happy as it was.

11

Saturday

The new creature eats too much fruit. We are going to run short, most likely. "We" again—that is *its* word; mine too, now, from hearing it so much. Good deal of fog this morning. I do not go out in the fog myself. The new creature does. It goes out in all weathers, and stumps right in with its muddy feet. And talks. It used to be so pleasant and quiet here.

13

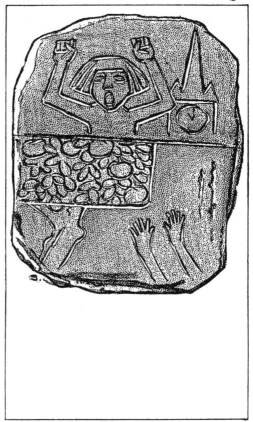

Extracts from Adam's Diary

Sunday

Pulled through. This day is getting to be more and more trying. It was selected and set apart last November as a day of rest. I already had six of them per week, before. This morning found the new creature trying to clod apples out of that forbidden tree.

Monday

The new creature says its name is
Eve. That is all right, I have no
objections. Says it is to call it by
when I want it to come. I said it
was superfluous, then. The word
evidently raised me in its respect;
and indeed it is a large, good word,
and will bear repetition. It says it
is not an It, it is a She. This is probably doubtful; yet it is all one to me;
what she is were nothing to me if she
would but go by herself and not talk.

Extracts from Adam's Diary

Tuesday

She has littered the whole estate with execrable names and offensive signs:

☞ THIS WAY TO THE WHIRLPOOL.

☞ THIS WAY TO GOAT ISLAND.

☞ CAVE OF THE WINDS THIS WAY.

She says this park would make a tidy summer resort, if there was any custom for it. Summer resort—another invention of hers—just words, without any meaning. What is a summer resort? But it is best not to ask her, she has such a rage for explaining.

19

Extracts from Adam's Diary

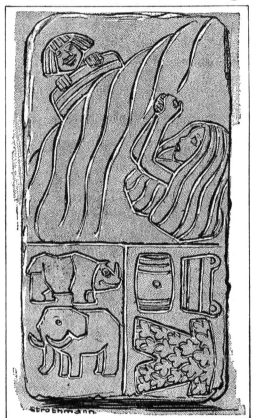

20

Friday

She has taken to beseeching me to stop going over the Falls. What harm does it do? Says it makes her shudder. I wonder why. I have always done it — always liked the plunge, and the excitement, and the coolness. I supposed it was what the Falls were for. They have no other use that I can see, and they must have been made for something. She says they were only made for scenery— like the rhinoceros and the mastodon.

I went over the Falls in a barrel— not satisfactory to her. Went over in a tub—still not satisfactory. Swam the Whirlpool and the Rapids in a fig-leaf suit. It got much damaged. Hence, tedious complaints about my extravagance. I am too much hampered here. What I need is change of scene.

21

Saturday

I escaped last Tuesday night, and
travelled two days, and built me another shelter, in a secluded place, and
obliterated my tracks as well as I
could, but she hunted me out by
means of a beast which she has tamed
and calls a wolf, and came making
that pitiful noise again, and shed-
ding that water out of the places she
looks with. I was obliged to return
with her, but will presently emigrate
again, when occasion offers. She en-
gages herself in many foolish things:
among others, trying to study out
why the animals called lions and
tigers live on grass and flowers, when,
as she says, the sort of teeth they
wear would indicate that they were
intended to eat each other. This is
foolish, because to do that would be

Saturday

to kill each other, and that would introduce what, as I understand it, is
called "death"; and death, as I have
been told, has not yet entered the
Park. Which is a pity, on some accounts.

Extracts from Adam's Diary

26

Extracts from Adam's Diary

Sunday

Pulled through.

27

Monday

I believe I see what the week is for: it is to give time to rest up from the weariness of Sunday. It seems a good idea. . . . She has been climbing that tree again. Clodded her out of it. She said nobody was looking. Seems to consider that a sufficient justification for chancing any dangerous thing. Told her that. The word justification moved her admiration— and envy too, I thought. It is a good word.

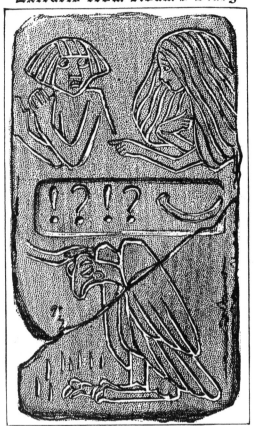

30

Thursday

She told me she was made out of a
rib taken from my body.   This is at
least doubtful, if not more than that.
I have not missed any rib. . . . She is
in much trouble about the buzzard;
says grass does not agree with it; is
afraid she can't raise it; thinks it was
intended to live on decayed flesh.
The buzzard must get along the best
it can with what is provided.   We
cannot overturn the whole scheme to
accommodate the buzzard.

31

Extracts from Adam's Diary

32

Saturday

She fell in the pond yesterday, when she was looking at herself in it, which she is always doing. She nearly strangled, and said it was most un. comfortable. This made her sorry for the creatures which live in there, which she calls fish, for she continues to fasten names on to things that don't need them and don't come when they are called by them, which is a matter of no consequence to her, as she is such a numskull anyway; so she got a lot of them out and brought them in last night and put them in my bed to keep warm, but I have noticed them now and then all day, and I don't see that they are any happier there than they were before, only quieter. When night comes I shall throw them out-doors. I will not

33

Extracts from Adam's Diary

34

Extracts from Adam's Diary

Saturday

sleep with them again, for I find them clammy and unpleasant to lie among when a person hasn't anything on.

36

Extracts from Adam's Diary

Sunday
    Pulled through.

38

Tuesday

She has taken up with a snake now. The other animals are glad, for she was always experimenting with them and bothering them; and I am glad, because the snake talks, and this enables me to get a rest.

4

39

Friday

She says the snake advises her to try the fruit of that tree, and says the result will be a great and fine and noble education. I told her there would be another result, too — it would introduce death into the world. That was a mistake—it had been better to keep the remark to myself; it only gave her an idea—she could save the sick buzzard, and furnish fresh meat to the despondent lions and tigers. I advised her to keep away from the tree. She said she wouldn't. I foresee trouble. Will emigrate.

Wednesday

I have had a variegated time. I escaped that night, and rode a horse all night as fast as he could go, hoping to get clear out of the Park and hide in some other country before the trouble should begin; but it was not to be. About an hour after sunup, as I was riding through a flowery plain where thousands of animals were grazing, slumbering, or playing with each other, according to their wont, all of a sudden they broke into a tempest of frightful noises, and in one moment the plain was in a frantic commotion and every beast was destroying its neighbor. I knew what it meant—Eve had eaten that fruit, and death was come into the world. . . . The tigers ate my horse, paying no attention when I ordered them to

43

Wednesday

desist, and they would even have eaten me if I had stayed—which I didn't, but went away in much haste. . . . I found this place, outside the Park, and was fairly comfortable for a few days, but she has found me out. Found me out, and has named the place Tonawanda—says it *looks* like that. In fact, I was not sorry she came, for there are but meagre pickings here, and she brought some of those apples. I was obliged to eat them, I was so hungry. It was against my principles, but I find that principles have no real force except when one is well fed. . . . She came curtained in boughs and bunches of leaves, and when I asked her what she meant by such nonsense, and snatched them away and threw them

45

46

Wednesday

down, she tittered and blushed. I
had never seen a person titter and
blush before, and to me it seemed un-
becoming and idiotic. She said I
would soon know how it was myself.
This was correct. Hungry as I was, I
laid down the apple half eaten—certainly the best one I ever saw, considering the lateness of the season—
and arrayed myself in the discarded
boughs and branches, and then spoke
to her with some severity and ordered
her to go and get some more and not
make such a spectacle of herself.
She did it, and after this we crept
down to where the wild-beast battle
had been, and collected some skins,
and I made her patch together a
couple of suits proper for public oc-
casions. They are uncomfortable, it

47

48

Wednesday

is true, but stylish, and that is the
main point about clothes. . . . I find
she is a good deal of a companion. I
see I should be lonesome and de-
pressed without her, now that I have
lost my property. Another thing,
she says it is ordered that we work
for our living hereafter. She will be
useful. I will superintend.

Ten Days Later

She accuses *me* of being the cause of our disaster! She says, with apparent sincerity and truth, that the Serpent assured her that the forbidden fruit was not apples, it was chestnuts. I said I was innocent, then, for I had not eaten any chestnuts. She said the Serpent informed her that "chestnut" was a figurative term meaning an aged and mouldy joke. I turned pale at that, for I have made many jokes to pass the weary time, and some of them could have been of that sort, though I had honestly supposed that they were new when I made them. She asked me if I had made one just at the time of the catastrophe. I was obliged to admit that I had made one to myself, though not aloud. It was this.

51

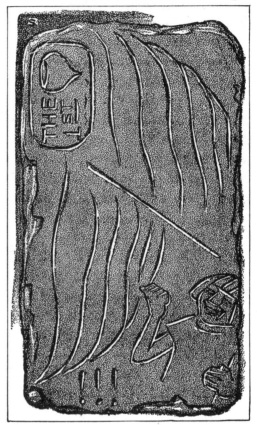

Ten Days Later

I was thinking about the Falls, and I said to myself, "How wonderful it is to see that vast body of water tumble down there!" Then in an instant a bright thought flashed into my head, and I let it fly, saying, "It would be a deal more wonderful to see it tumble *up* there!"—and I was just about to kill myself with laughing at it when all nature broke loose in war and death, and I had to flee for my life. "There," she said, with triumph, "that is just it; the Serpent mentioned that very jest, and called it the First Chestnut, and said it was coeval with the creation." Alas, I am indeed to blame. Would that I were not witty; oh, would that I had never had that radiant thought!

53

54

Next Year

We have named it Cain. She
caught it while I was up country
trapping on the North Shore of the
Erie; caught it in the timber a couple
of miles from our dug-out — or it
might have been four, she isn't certain which. It resembles us in some
ways, and may be a relation. That
is what she thinks, but this is an error,
in my judgment. The difference in
size warrants the conclusion that it
is a different and new kind of animal
—a fish, perhaps, though when I put
it in the water to see, it sank, and she
plunged in and snatched it out before
there was opportunity for the experiment to determine the matter.
I still think it is a fish, but she is indifferent about what it is, and will
not let me have it to try. I do not

Next Year

understand this. The coming of the
creature seems to have changed her
whole nature and made her unrea-
sonable about experiments. She
thinks more of it than she does of any
of the other animals, but is not able
to explain why. Her mind is dis-
ordered—everything shows it. Sometimes she carries the fish in her arms
half the night when it complains and
wants to get to the water. At such
times the water comes out of the
places in her face that she looks out
of, and she pats the fish on the back
and makes soft sounds with her
mouth to soothe it, and betrays sorrow and solicitude in a hundred ways.
I have never seen her do like this
with any other fish, and it troubles
me greatly. She used to carry the

57

Next Year

young tigers around so, and play
with them, before we lost our property; but it was only play; she never
took on about them like this when
their dinner disagreed with them.

Extracts from Adam's Diary

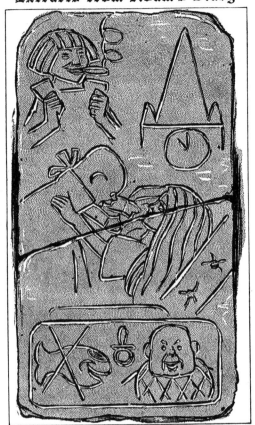

60

Sunday

She doesn't work Sundays, but lies around all tired out, and likes to have the fish wallow over her; and she makes fool noises to amuse it, and pretends to chew its paws, and that makes it laugh. I have not seen a fish before that could laugh. This makes me doubt. . . . I have come to like Sunday myself. Superintending all the week tires a body so. There ought to be more Sundays. In the old days they were tough, but now they come handy.

61

Wednesday

It isn't a fish. I cannot quite make out what it is. It makes curious, devilish noises when not satisfied, and says "goo-goo" when it is. It is not one of us, for it doesn't walk; it is not a bird, for it doesn't fly; it is not a frog, for it doesn't hop; it is not a snake, for it doesn't crawl; I feel sure it is not a fish, though I cannot get a chance to find out whether it can swim or not. It merely lies around, and mostly on its back, with its feet up. I have not seen any other animal do that before. I said I believed it was an enigma, but she only admired the word without understanding it. In my judgment it is either an enigma or some kind of a bug. If it dies, I will take it apart and see what its arrangements are. I never had a thing perplex me so.

Three Months Later

The perplexity augments instead of diminishing. I sleep but little. It has ceased from lying around, and goes about on its four legs now. Yet it differs from the other four-legged animals in that its front legs are unusually short, consequently this causes the main part of its person to stick up uncomfortably high in the air, and this is not attractive. It is built much as we are, but its method of travelling shows that it is not of our breed. The short front legs and long hind ones indicate that it is of the kangaroo family, but it is a marked variation of the species, since the true kangaroo hops, whereas this one never does. Still, it is a curious and interesting variety, and has not been catalogued before. As I dis-

Three Months Later

covered it, I have felt justified in securing the credit of the discovery by attaching my name to it, and hence have called it *Kangaroorum Adamiensis.* . . . It must have been a young one when it came, for it has grown exceedingly since. It must be five times as big, now, as it was then, and when discontented is able to make from twenty-two to thirty-eight times the noise it made at first. Coercion does not modify this, but has the contrary effect. For this reason I discontinued the system. She reconciles it by persuasion, and by giving it things which she had previously told it she wouldn't give it. As already observed, I was not at home when it first came, and she told me she found it in the woods. It seems

67

Three Months Later

odd that it should be the only one,
yet it must be so, for I have worn
myself out these many weeks trying
to find another one to add to my
collection, and for this one to play
with; for surely then it would be
quieter, and we could tame it more
easily. But I find none, nor any
vestige of any; and strangest of all,
no tracks. It has to live on the
ground, it cannot help itself; therefore, how does it get about without
leaving a track? I have set a dozen
traps, but they do no good. I catch
all small animals except that one;
animals that merely go into the trap
out of curiosity, I think, to see what
the milk is there for. They never
drink it.

69

Three Months Later

The kangaroo still continues to grow, which is very strange and perplexing. I never knew one to be so long getting its growth. It has fur on its head now; not like kangaroo fur, but exactly like our hair, except that it is much finer and softer, and instead of being black is red. I am like to lose my mind over the capricious and harassing developments of this unclassifiable zoological freak. If I could catch another one—but that is hopeless; it is a new variety, and the only sample; this is plain. But I caught a true kangaroo and brought it in, thinking that this one, being lonesome, would rather have that for company than have no kin at all, or any animal it could feel a nearness to or get sympathy from in

Three Months Later

its forlorn condition here among strangers who do not know its ways or habits, or what to do to make it feel that it is among friends; but it was a mistake—it went into such fits at the sight of the kangaroo that I was convinced it had never seen one before. I pity the poor noisy little animal, but there is nothing I can do to make it happy. If I could tame it—but that is out of the question; the more I try, the worse I seem to make it. It grieves me to the heart to see it in its little storms of sorrow and passion. I wanted to let it go, but she wouldn't hear of it. That seemed cruel and not like her; and yet she may be right. It might be lonelier than ever; for since I cannot find another one, how could *it?*

73

74

Extracts from Adam's Diary

Five Months Later

It is not a kangaroo. No, for it
supports itself by holding to her finger, and thus goes a few steps on its
hind legs, and then falls down. It is
probably some kind of a bear; and
yet it has no tail—as yet—and no fur,
except on its head. It still keeps on
growing—that is a curious circum-
stance, for bears get their growth
earlier than this. Bears are dangerous — since our catastrophe — and I
shall not be satisfied to have this
one prowling about the place much
longer without a muzzle on. I have
offered to get her a kangaroo if she
would let this one go, but it did no
good — she is determined to run us
into all sorts of foolish risks, I think.
She was not like this before she lost
her mind.

75

Extracts from Adam's Diary

A Fortnight Later

I examined its mouth. There is no danger yet; it has only one tooth. It has no tail yet. It makes more noise now than it ever did before — and mainly at night. I have moved out. But I shall go over, mornings, to breakfast, and to see if it has more teeth. If it gets a mouthful of teeth, it will be time for it to go, tail or no tail, for a bear does not need a tail in order to be dangerous.

77

Extracts from Adam's Diary

Four Months Later

I have been off hunting and fishing a month, up in the region that she calls Buffalo; I don't know why, unless it is because there are not any buffaloes there. Meantime the bear has learned to paddle around all by itself on its hind legs, and says "poppa" and "momma." It is certainly a new species. This resemblance to words may be purely accidental, of course, and may have no purpose or meaning; but even in that case it is still extraordinary, and is a thing which no other bear can do. This imitation of speech, taken together with general absence of fur and entire absence of tail, sufficiently indicates that this is a new kind of bear. The further study of it will be exceedingly interesting. Meantime I will go off

80

Four Months Later

on a far expedition among the forests
of the North and make an exhaustive
search.   There must certainly be another one somewhere, and this one
will be less dangerous when it has
company of its own species.   I will
go straightway; but I will muzzle this
one first.

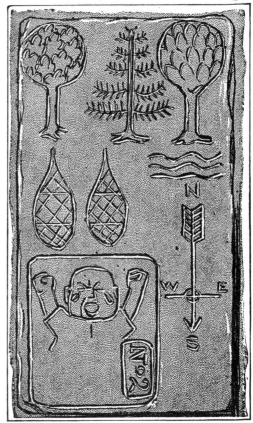

82

Three Months Later

It has been a weary, weary hunt, yet I have had no success. In the mean time, without stirring from the home estate, she has caught another one! I never saw such luck. I might have hunted these woods a hundred years, I never should have run across that thing.

83

Next Day

I have been comparing the new one with the old one, and it is perfectly plain that they are the same breed. I was going to stuff one of them for my collection, but she is prejudiced against it for some reason or other; so I have relinquished the idea, though I think it is a mistake. It would be an irreparable loss to science if they should get away. The old one is tamer than it was, and can laugh and talk like the parrot, having learned this, no doubt, from being with the parrot so much, and having the imitative faculty in a highly developed degree. I shall be astonished if it turns out to be a new kind of parrot; and yet I ought not to be astonished, for it has already been everything else it could think of, since those

85

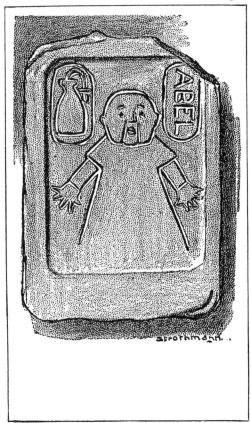

Next Day

first days when it was a fish. The
new one is as ugly now as the old one
was at first; has the same sulphur-
and-raw-meat complexion and the
same singular head without any fur
on it. She calls it Abel.

7

87

88

Ten Years Later

They are boys; we found it out long ago. It was their coming in that small, immature shape that puzzled us; we were not used to it. There are some girls now. Abel is a good boy, but if Cain had stayed a bear it would have improved him. After all these years, I see that I was mistaken about Eve in the beginning; it is better to live outside the Garden with her than inside it without her. At first I thought she talked too much; but now I should be sorry to have that voice fall silent and pass out of my life. Blessed be the chestnut that brought us near together and taught me to know the goodness of her heart and the sweetness of her spirit!

THE END

89

EVE'S DIARY

EVE'S DIARY
—
MARK TWAIN

Eve's Diary

Eve's Diary

TRANSLATED FROM THE ORIGINAL MS.

By Mark Twain

ILLUSTRATED BY
LESTER RALPH

LONDON AND NEW YORK
HARPER & BROTHERS
PUBLISHERS :: MCMVI

Eve's Diary

Translated from the Original

Eve's Diary

Translated from the Original

Saturday

I am almost a whole day old, now. I arrived yesterday. That is as it seems to me. And it must be so, for if there was a day-before-yesterday I was not there when it happened, or I should remember it. It could be, of course, that it did happen, and that I was not noticing. Very well; I will be very watchful, now, and if any day-before-yesterdays happen I will make a note of it. It will be best to start right and not let the record get confused, for some instinct tells me that these details are going to be important to the historian some day.

3

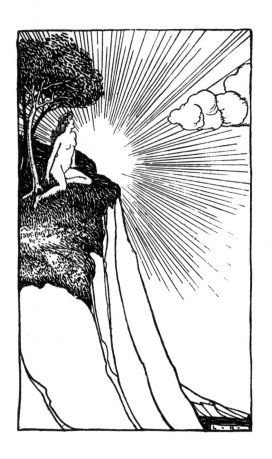

Saturday

For I feel like an experiment, I feel exactly like an experiment; it would be impossible for a person to feel more like an experiment than I do, and so I am coming to feel convinced that that is what I *am* — an experiment; just an experiment, and nothing more.

Then if I am an experiment, am I the whole of it? No, I think not; I think the rest of it is part of it. I am the main part of it, but I think the rest of it has its share in the matter. Is my position assured, or do I have to watch it and take care of it? The latter, perhaps. Some instinct tells me that eternal vigilance is the price of supremacy. [That is a good phrase, I think, for one so young.]

Everything looks better to - day than it did yesterday. In the rush

5

Saturday

of finishing up yesterday, the mountains were left in a ragged condition, and some of the plains were so cluttered with rubbish and remnants that the aspects were quite distressing. Noble and beautiful works of art should not be subjected to haste; and this majestic new world is indeed a most noble and beautiful work. And certainly marvellously near to being perfect, notwithstanding the shortness of the time. There are too many stars in some places and not enough in others, but that can be remedied presently, no doubt. The moon got loose last night, and slid down and fell out of the scheme—a very great loss; it breaks my heart to think of it. There isn't another thing among the ornaments and dec-

Saturday

orations that is comparable to it for beauty and finish. It should have been fastened better. If we can only get it back again—

But of course there is no telling where it went to. And besides, whoever gets it will hide it; I know it because I would do it myself. I believe I can be honest in all other matters, but I already begin to realize that the core and centre of my nature is love of the beautiful, a passion for the beautiful, and that it would not be safe to trust me with a moon that belonged to another person and that person didn't know I had it. I could give up a moon that I found in the daytime, because I should be afraid some one was looking; but if I found it in the dark, I am sure I should find

9

Saturday

some kind of an excuse for not saying anything about it. For I do love moons, they are so pretty and so romantic. I wish we had five or six; I would never go to bed; I should never get tired lying on the moss-bank and looking up at them.

Stars are good, too. I wish I could get some to put in my hair. But I suppose I never can. You would be surprised to find how far off they are, for they do not look it. When they first showed, last night, I tried to knock some down with a pole, but it didn't reach, which astonished me; then I tried clods till I was all tired out, but I never got one. It was because I am left-handed and cannot throw good. Even when I aimed at the one I wasn't after I couldn't hit

11

Saturday

the other one, though I did make some close shots, for I saw the black blot of the clod sail right into the midst of the golden clusters forty or fifty times, just barely missing them, and if I could have held out a little longer maybe I could have got one.

So I cried a little, which was natural, I suppose, for one of my age, and after I was rested I got a basket and started for a place on the extreme rim of the circle, where the stars were close to the ground and I could get them with my hands, which would be better, anyway, because I could gather them tenderly then, and not break them. But it was farther than I thought, and at last I had to give it up; I was so tired I couldn't drag my feet another step; and be-

13

Saturday

sides, they were sore and hurt me
very much.

I couldn't get back home; it was
too far, and turning cold; but I found
some tigers, and nestled in among
them and was most adorably comfortable, and their breath was sweet
and pleasant, because they live on
strawberries. I had never seen a
tiger before, but I knew them in a
minute by the stripes. If I could
have one of those skins, it would
make a lovely gown.

To-day I am getting better ideas
about distances. I was so eager to
get hold of every pretty thing that I
giddily grabbed for it, sometimes
when it was too far off, and sometimes when it was but six inches
away but seemed a foot—alas, with

15

Saturday

thorns between! I learned a lesson;
also I made an axiom, all out of my
own head — my very first one: *The
scratched Experiment shuns the thorn.*
I think it is a very good one for one
so young.

I followed the other Experiment
around, yesterday afternoon, at a
distance, to see what it might be for,
if I could. But I was not able to
make out. I think it is a man. I
had never seen a man, but it looked
like one, and I feel sure that that is
what it is. I realize that I feel more
curiosity about it than about any
of the other reptiles. If it is a reptile,
and I suppose it is; for it has frowsy
hair and blue eyes, and looks like a
reptile. It has no hips; it tapers like
a carrot; when it stands, it spreads

17

Saturday

itself apart like a derrick; so I think
it is a reptile, though it may be
architecture.

I was afraid of it at first, and started to run every time it turned around,
for I thought it was going to chase me;
but by-and-by I found it was only
trying to get away, so after that I
was not timid any more, but tracked
it along, several hours, about twenty
yards behind, which made it nervous
and unhappy. At last it was a good
deal worried, and climbed a tree. I
waited a good while, then gave it up
and went home.

To-day the same thing over. I've
got it up the tree again.

19

Sunday

It is up there yet. Resting, apparently. But that is a subterfuge: Sunday isn't the day of rest; Saturday is appointed for that. It looks to me like a creature that is more interested in resting than in anything else. It would tire me to rest so much. It tires me just to sit around and watch the tree. I do wonder what it is for; I never see it do anything.

They returned the moon last night, and I was *so* happy! I think it is very honest of them. It slid down and fell off again, but I was not distressed; there is no need to worry when one has that kind of neighbors; they will fetch it back. I wish I could do something to show my appreciation. I would like to send

21

Sunday

them some stars, for we have more
than we can use. I mean I, not we,
for I can see that the reptile cares
nothing for such things.

It has low tastes, and is not kind.
When I went there yesterday evening in the gloaming it had crept down
and was trying to catch the little
speckled fishes that play in the pool,
and I had to clod it to make it go
up the tree again and let them alone.
I wonder if *that* is what it is for?
Hasn't it any heart? Hasn't it any
compassion for those little creatures?
Can it be that it was designed and
manufactured for such ungentle work?
It has the look of it. One of the
clods took it back of the ear, and it
used language. It gave me a thrill,
for it was the first time I had ever

Sunday

heard speech, except my own.   I did
not understand the words, but they
seemed expressive.

When I found it could talk, I felt a
new interest in it, for I love to talk; I
talk all day, and in my sleep, too, and
I am very interesting, but if I had
another to talk to I could be twice as
interesting, and would never stop, if
desired.

If this reptile is a man, it isn't an
it, is it?   That wouldn't be gram-
matical, would it?   I think it would
be *he*.   I think so.   In that case one
would parse it thus: nominative, *he;*
dative, *him;* possessive, *his'n*.   Well,
I will consider it a man and call it
he until it turns out to be something
else.   This will be handier than having so many uncertainties.

25

Next week Sunday

All the week I tagged around after him and tried to get acquainted. I had to do the talking, because he was shy, but I didn't mind it. He seemed pleased to have me around, and I used the sociable "we" a good deal, because it seemed to flatter him to be included.

27

Wednesday

We are getting along very well
indeed, now, and getting better and
better acquainted. He does not try
to avoid me any more, which is a
good sign, and shows that he likes to
have me with him. That pleases
me, and I study to be useful to him in
every way I can, so as to increase his
regard. During the last day or two
I have taken all the work of naming
things off his hands, and this has been
a great relief to him, for he has no
gift in that line, and is evidently
very grateful. He can't think of a
rational name to save him, but I do
not let him see that I am aware of
his defect. Whenever a new creature
comes along, I name it before he has
time to expose himself by an awk-
ward silence. In this way I have

29

Wednesday

saved him many embarrassments.
I have no defect like his. The minute I set eyes on an animal I know
what it is. I don't have to reflect a
moment; the right name comes out
instantly, just as if it were an in-
spiration, as no doubt it is, for I am
sure it wasn't in me half a minute
before. I seem to know just by the
shape of the creature and the way
it acts what animal it is.

When the dodo came along he
thought it was a wildcat—I saw it in
his eye. But I saved him. And I
was careful not to do it in a way
that could hurt his pride. I just
spoke up in a quite natural way of
pleased surprise, and not as if I was
dreaming of conveying information,
and said, "Well, I do declare if there

31

Wednesday

isn't the dodo!" I explained—without seeming to be explaining—how I knew it for a dodo, and although I thought maybe he was a little piqued that I knew the creature when he didn't, it was quite evident that he admired me. That was very agreeable, and I thought of it more than once with gratification before I slept. How little a thing can make us happy when we feel that we have earned it.

33

Thursday

My first sorrow. Yesterday he avoided me and seemed to wish I would not talk to him. I could not believe it, and thought there was some mistake, for I loved to be with him, and loved to hear him talk, and so how could it be that he could feel unkind towards me when I had not done anything? But at last it seemed true, so I went away and sat lonely in the place where I first saw him the morning that we were made and I did not know what he was and was indifferent about him; but now it was a mournful place, and every little thing spoke of him, and my heart was very sore. I did not know why very clearly, for it was a new feeling; I had not experienced it before, and it was all a mys-

35

Thursday

tery, and I could not make it out.

But when night came I could not bear the lonesomeness, and went to the new shelter which he has built, to ask him what I had done that was wrong and how I could mend it and get back his kindness again; but he put me out in the rain, and it was my first sorrow.

Sunday

It is pleasant again, now, and I am happy; but those were heavy days; I do not think of them when I can help it.

I tried to get him some of those apples, but I cannot learn to throw straight. I failed, but I think the good intention pleased him. They are forbidden, and he says I shall come to harm; but so I come to harm through pleasing him, why shall I care for that harm?

Monday

This morning I told him my name, hoping it would interest him. But he did not care for it. It is strange. If he should tell me his name, I would care. I think it would be pleasanter in my ears than any other sound.

He talks very little. Perhaps it is because he is not bright, and is sensitive about it and wishes to conceal it. It is such a pity that he should feel so, for brightness is nothing; it is in the heart that the values lie. I wish I could make him understand that a loving good heart is riches, and riches enough, and that without it intellect is poverty.

Although he talks so little he has quite a considerable vocabulary. This morning he used a surprisingly good word. He evidently recognized, him-

41

Monday

self, that it was a good one, for he worked it in twice afterwards, casually. It was not good casual art, still it showed that he possesses a certain quality of perception. Without a doubt that seed can be made to grow, if cultivated.

Where did he get that word? I do not think I have ever used it.

No, he took no interest in my name. I tried to hide my disappointment, but I suppose I did not succeed. I went away and sat on the moss-bank with my feet in the water. It is where I go when I hunger for companionship, some one to look at, some one to talk to. It is not enough—that lovely white body painted there in the pool—but it is something, and something is better than utter loneliness.

43

Monday

It talks when I talk; it is sad when
I am sad; it comforts me with its
sympathy; it says, "Do not be down-
hearted, you poor friendless girl; I
will be your friend." It *is* a good
friend to me, and my only one; it is
my sister.

That first time that she forsook me!
ah, I shall never forget that—never,
never. My heart was lead in my
body! I said, "She was all I had,
and now she is gone!" In my despair I said, "Break, my heart; I cannot bear my life any more!" and hid
my face in my hands, and there was
no solace for me. And when I took
them away, after a little, there she
was again, white and shining and
beautiful, and I sprang into her arms!

That was perfect happiness; I had

45

Monday

known happiness before, but it was
not like this, which was ecstasy. I
never doubted her afterwards. Sometimes she stayed away—maybe an
hour, maybe almost the whole day,
but I waited and did not doubt; I
said, "She is busy, or she is gone a
journey, but she will come." And it
was so: she always did. At night she
would not come if it was dark, for
she was a timid little thing; but if
there was a moon she would come.
I am not afraid of the dark, but she
is younger than I am; she was born
after I was. Many and many are the
visits I have paid her; she is my comfort and my refuge when my life is
hard—and it is mainly that.

47

Tuesday

All the morning I was at work improving the estate; and I purposely kept away from him in the hope that he would get lonely and come. But he did not.

At noon I stopped for the day and took my recreation by flitting all about with the bees and the butterflies and revelling in the flowers, those beautiful creatures that catch the smile of God out of the sky and preserve it! I gathered them, and made them into wreaths and garlands and clothed myself in them while I ate my luncheon—apples, of course; then I sat in the shade and wished and waited. But he did not come.

But no matter. Nothing would have come of it, for he does not care

49

Tuesday

for flowers. He calls them rubbish, and cannot tell one from another, and thinks it is superior to feel like that. He does not care for me, he does not care for flowers, he does not care for the painted sky at eventide—is there anything he does care for, except building shacks to coop himself up in from the good clean rain, and thumping the melons, and sampling the grapes, and fingering the fruit on the trees, to see how those properties are coming along?

I laid a dry stick on the ground and tried to bore a hole in it with another one, in order to carry out a scheme that I had, and soon I got an awful fright. A thin, transparent, bluish film rose out of the hole, and I dropped everything and ran! I thought it

51

Tuesday

was a spirit, and I *was* so frightened!
But I looked back, and it was not
coming; so I leaned against a rock
and rested and panted, and let my
limbs go on trembling until they got
steady again; then I crept warily
back, alert, watching, and ready to
fly if there was occasion; and when I
was come near, I parted the branches
of a rose-bush and peeped through
—wishing the man was about, I was
looking so cunning and pretty—but
the sprite was gone. I went there,
and there was a pinch of delicate pink
dust in the hole. I put my finger in,
to feel it, and said *ouch!* and took
it out again. It was a cruel pain. I
put my finger in my mouth; and by
standing first on one foot and then
the other, and grunting, I presently

53

Tuesday

eased my misery; then I was full of
interest, and began to examine.

I was curious to know what the
pink dust was. Suddenly the name
of it occurred to me, though I had
never heard of it before. It was *fire!*
I was as certain of it as a person could
be of anything in the world. So
without hesitation I named it that—
fire.

I had created something that didn't
exist before; I had added a new thing
to the world's uncountable properties;
I realized this, and was proud of my
achievement, and was going to run
and find him and tell him about it,
thinking to raise myself in his esteem
—but I reflected, and did not do it.
No—he would not care for it. He
would ask what it was good for, and

Tuesday

what could I answer? For if it was
not *good* for something, but only
beautiful, merely beautiful—

So I sighed, and did not go. For
it wasn't good for anything; it could
not build a shack, it could not improve melons, it could not hurry a
fruit crop; it was useless, it was a
foolishness and a vanity; he would
despise it and say cutting words.
But to me it was not despicable; I
said, "Oh, you fire, I love you, you
dainty pink creature, for you are
beautiful—and that is enough!" and
was going to gather it to my breast.
But refrained. Then I made another
maxim out of my own head, though
it was so nearly like the first one that
I was afraid it was only a plagiarism:
"*The burnt Experiment shuns the fire.*"

57

Tuesday

I wrought again; and when I had made a good deal of fire-dust I emptied it into a handful of dry brown grass, intending to carry it home and keep it always and play with it; but the wind struck it and it sprayed up and spat out at me fiercely, and I dropped it and ran. When I looked back the blue spirit was towering up and stretching and rolling away like a cloud, and instantly I thought of the name of it—*smoke!*—though, upon my word, I had never heard of smoke before.

Soon, brilliant yellow-and-red flares shot up through the smoke, and I named them in an instant—*flames!*—and I was right, too, though these were the very first flames that had ever been in the world. They climb-

59

Tuesday

ed the trees, they flashed splendidly
in and out of the vast and increasing
volume of tumbling smoke, and I had
to clap my hands and laugh and
dance in my rapture, it was so new
and strange and so wonderful and so
beautiful!

He came running, and stopped and
gazed, and said not a word for many
minutes. Then he asked what it was.
Ah, it was too bad that he should ask
such a direct question. I had to answer it, of course, and I did. I said
it was fire. If it annoyed him that
I should know and he must ask, that
was not my fault; I had no desire to
annoy him. After a pause he asked:

"How did it come?"

Another direct question, and it also
had to have a direct answer.

Tuesday

"I made it."

The fire was travelling farther and farther off. He went to the edge of the burned place and stood looking down, and said:

"What are these?"

"Fire-coals."

He picked up one to examine it, but changed his mind and put it down again. Then he went away. *Nothing* interests him.

But I was interested. There were ashes, gray and soft and delicate and pretty—I knew what they were at once. And the embers; I knew the embers, too. I found my apples, and raked them out, and was glad; for I am very young and my appetite is active. But I was disappointed; they were all burst open and spoiled.

63

Tuesday

Spoiled apparently; but it was not
so; they were better than raw ones.
Fire is beautiful; some day it will be
useful, I think.

Friday

I saw him again, for a moment, last Monday at nightfall, but only for a moment. I was hoping he would praise me for trying to improve the estate, for I had meant well and had worked hard. But he was not pleased, and turned away and left me. He was also displeased on another account: I tried once more to persuade him to stop going over the Falls. That was because the fire had revealed to me a new passion—quite new, and distinctly different from love, grief, and those others which I had already discovered—*fear*. And it is horrible!—I wish I had never discovered it; it gives me dark moments, it spoils my happiness, it makes me shiver and tremble and shudder. But I could not persuade

67

Friday

him, for he has not discovered fear yet, and so he could not understand me.

Extract from Adam's Diary

Perhaps I ought to remember that she is very young, a mere girl, and make allowances. She is all interest, eagerness, vivacity, the world is to her a charm, a wonder, a mystery, a joy; she can't speak for delight when she finds a new flower, she must pet it and caress it and smell it and talk to it, and pour out endearing names upon it. And she is color-mad: brown rocks, yellow sand, gray moss, green foliage, blue sky; the pearl of the dawn, the purple shadows on the mountains, the golden islands floating in crimson seas at sunset, the pallid moon sailing through the shredded cloud-rack, the

69

Friday

star-jewels glittering in the wastes of
space—none of them is of any prac-
tical value, so far as I can see, but because they have color and majesty,
that is enough for her, and she loses
her mind over them. If she could
quiet down and keep still a couple of
minutes at a time, it would be a re-
poseful spectacle. In that case I think
I could enjoy looking at her; indeed I
am sure I could, for I am coming to
realize that she is a quite remarkably
comely creature—lithe, slender, trim,
rounded, shapely, nimble, graceful;
and once when she was standing
marble-white and sun-drenched on a
bowlder, with her young head tilted
back and her hand shading her eyes,
watching the flight of a bird in the
sky, I recognized that she was beautiful.

Monday noon.—If there is any-

Friday

thing on the planet that she is not interested in it is not in my list. There are animals that I am indifferent to, but it is not so with her. She has no discrimination, she takes to all of them, she thinks they are all treasures, every new one is welcome.

When the mighty brontosaurus came striding into camp, she regarded it as an acquisition, I considered it a calamity; that is a good sample of the lack of harmony that prevails in our views of things. She wanted to domesticate it, I wanted to make it a present of the homestead and move out. She believed it could be tamed by kind treatment and would be a good pet; I said a pet twenty-one feet high and eighty-four feet long would be no proper thing to have about the place, because, even with the best intentions and without meaning any harm, it

73

Friday

could sit down on the house and mash it, for any one could see by the look of its eye that it was absent-minded.

Still, her heart was set upon having that monster, and she couldn't give it up. She thought we could start a dairy with it, and wanted me to help her milk it; but I wouldn't; it was too risky. The sex wasn't right, and we hadn't any ladder anyway. Then she wanted to ride it, and look at the scenery. Thirty or forty feet of its tail was lying on the ground, like a fallen tree, and she thought she could climb it, but she was mistaken; when she got to the steep place it was too slick and down she came, and would have hurt herself but for me.

Was she satisfied now? No. Nothing ever satisfies her but demonstration; untested theories are not in her line, and she won't have them. It is the right spirit, I concede it; it attracts

75

Friday

me; I feel the influence of it; if I were with her more I think I should take it up myself. Well, she had one theory remaining about this colossus: she thought that if we could tame him and make him friendly we could stand him in the river and use him for a bridge. It turned out that he was already plenty tame enough—at least as far as she was concerned—so she tried her theory, but it failed; every time she got him properly placed in the river and went ashore to cross over on him, he came out and followed her around like a pet mountain. Like the other animals. They all do that.

Tuesday — Wednesday — Thursday —and to-day: all without seeing him. It is a long time to be alone; still, it is better to be alone than unwelcome.

77

Friday

I *had* to have company — I was made for it, I think — so I made friends with the animals. They are just charming, and they have the kindest disposition and the politest ways; they never look sour, they never let you feel that you are intruding, they smile at you and wag their tail, if they've got one, and they are always ready for a romp or an excursion or anything you want to propose. I think they are perfect gentlemen. All these days we have had such good times, and it hasn't been lonesome for me, ever. Lonesome! No, I should say not. Why, there's always a swarm of them around—sometimes as much as four or five acres—you can't count them; and when you stand on a rock in the

Friday

midst and look out over the furry
expanse, it is so mottled and splashed
and gay with color and frisking sheen
and sun-flash, and so rippled with
stripes, that you might think it was
a lake, only you know it isn't; and
there's storms of sociable birds, and
hurricanes of whirring wings; and
when the sun strikes all that feathery
commotion, you have a blazing up of
all the colors you can think of, enough
to put your eyes out.

We have made long excursions,
and I have seen a great deal of the
world—almost all of it, I think; and
so I am the first traveller, and the
only one. When we are on the
march, it is an imposing sight—there's
nothing like it anywhere. For comfort I ride a tiger or a leopard, be-

81

Friday

cause it is soft and has a round back
that fits me, and because they are
such pretty animals; but for long distance or for scenery I ride the elephant. He hoists me up with his
trunk, but I can get off myself; when
we are ready to camp, he sits and I
slide down the back way.

The birds and animals are all
friendly to each other, and there are
no disputes about anything. They all
talk, and they all talk to me, but it
must be a foreign language, for I cannot make out a word they say; yet
they often understand me when I talk
back, particularly the dog and the
elephant. It makes me ashamed.
It shows that they are brighter than
I am, and are therefore my superiors.
It annoys me, for I want to be the

83

Friday

principal Experiment myself—and I intend to be, too.

I have learned a number of things, and am educated, now, but I wasn't at first. I was ignorant at first. At first it used to vex me because, with all my watching, I was never smart enough to be around when the water was running up-hill; but now I do not mind it. I have experimented and experimented until now I know it never does run up-hill, except in the dark. I know it does in the dark, because the pool never goes dry; which it would, of course, if the water didn't come back in the night. It is best to prove things by actual experiment; then you *know;* whereas if you depend on guessing and supposing and conjecturing, you will never get educated.

Friday

Some things you *can't* find out; but you will never know you can't by guessing and supposing: no, you have to be patient and go on experimenting until you find out that you can't find out. And it is delightful to have it that way, it makes the world so interesting. If there wasn't anything to find out, it would be dull. Even trying to find out and not finding out is just as interesting as trying to find out and finding out, and I don't know but more so. The secret of the water was a treasure until I *got* it; then the excitement all went away, and I recognized a sense of loss.

By experiment I know that wood swims, and dry leaves, and feathers, and plenty of other things; therefore by all that cumulative evidence you

7   87

Friday

know that a rock will swim; but you have to put up with simply knowing it, for there isn't any way to prove it —up to now. But I shall find a way —then *that* excitement will go. Such things make me sad; because by-and-by when I have found out everything there won't be any more excitements, and I do love excitements so! The other night I couldn't sleep for thinking about it.

At first I couldn't make out what I was made for, but now I think it was to search out the secrets of this wonderful world and be happy and thank the Giver of it all for devising it. I think there are many things to learn yet—I hope so; and by economizing and not hurrying too fast I think they will last weeks and weeks. I hope so.

89

Friday

When you cast up a feather it sails away on the air and goes out of sight; then you throw up a clod and it doesn't. It comes down, every time. I have tried it and tried it, and it is always so. I wonder why it is? Of course it *doesn't* come down, but why should it *seem* to? I suppose it is an optical illusion. I mean, one of them is. I don't know which one. It may be the feather, it may be the clod; I can't prove which it is, I can only demonstrate that one or the other is a fake, and let a person take his choice.

By watching, I know that the stars are not going to last. I have seen some of the best ones melt and run down the sky. Since one can melt, they can all melt; since they can all

Friday

melt, they can all melt the same
night. That sorrow will come — I
know it. I mean to sit up every
night and look at them as long as I
can keep awake; and I will impress
those sparkling fields on my memory,
so that by-and-by when they are
taken away I can by my fancy restore
those lovely myriads to the black sky
and make them sparkle again, and
double them by the blur of my tears.

93

After the Fall

When I look back, the Garden is a dream to me. It was beautiful, surpassingly beautiful, enchantingly beautiful; and now it is lost, and I shall not see it any more.

The Garden is lost, but I have found *him*, and am content. He loves me as well as he can; I love him with all the strength of my passionate nature, and this, I think, is proper to my youth and sex. If I ask myself why I love him, I find I do not know, and do not really much care to know; so I suppose that this kind of love is not a product of reasoning and statistics, like one's love for other reptiles and animals. I think that this must be so. I love certain birds because of their song; but I do not love Adam on account of his singing—no, it is not that;

95

After the Fall

the more he sings the more I do not
get reconciled to it. Yet I ask him to
sing, because I wish to learn to like
everything he is interested in. I am
sure I can learn, because at first I
could not stand it, but now I can. It
sours the milk, but it doesn't matter;
I can get used to that kind of milk.

It is not on account of his brightness that I love him—no, it is not that.
He is not to blame for his brightness,
such as it is, for he did not make it
himself; he is as God made him, and
that is sufficient. There was a wise
purpose in it; *that* I know. In time
it will develop, though I think it will
not be sudden; and, besides, there is
no hurry; he is well enough just as
he is.

It is not on account of his gracious

97

After the Fall

and considerate ways and his delicacy
that I love him.   No, he has lacks in
these regards, but he is well enough
just so, and is improving.

It is not on account of his industry
that I love him—no, it is not that.   I
think he has it in him, and I do not
know why he conceals it from me.
It is my only pain.   Otherwise he is
frank and open with me, now.   I am
sure he keeps nothing from me but
this.   It grieves me that he should
have a secret from me, and sometimes
it spoils my sleep, thinking of it, but
I will put it out of my mind; it shall
not trouble my happiness, which is
otherwise full to overflowing.

It is not on account of his education
that I love him—no, it is not that.
He is self-educated, and does really

99

After the Fall

know a multitude of things, but they are not so.

It is not on account of his chivalry that I love him—no, it is not that. He told on me, but I do not blame him; it is a peculiarity of sex, I think, and he did not make his sex. Of course I would not have told on him, I would have perished first; but that is a peculiarity of sex, too, and I do not take credit for it, for I did not make my sex.

Then why is it that I love him? *Merely because he is masculine,* I think.

At bottom he is good, and I love him for that, but I could love him without it. If he should beat me and abuse me, I should go on loving him. I know it. It is a matter of sex, I think.

101

After the Fall

He is strong and handsome, and I love him for that, and I admire him and am proud of him, but I could love him without those qualities. If he were plain, I should love him; if he were a wreck, I should love him; and I would work for him, and slave over him, and pray for him, and watch by his bedside until I died.

Yes, I think I love him merely because he is *mine* and is *masculine*. There is no other reason, I suppose. And so I think it is as I first said: that this kind of love is not a product of reasonings and statistics. It just *comes*—none knows whence—and cannot explain itself. And doesn't need to.

It is what I think. But I am only a girl, and the first that has examined

After the Fall

this matter, and it may turn out that in my ignorance and inexperience I have not got it right.

Forty Years Later

It is my prayer, it is my longing, that we may pass from this life together—a longing which shall never perish from the earth, but shall have place in the heart of every wife that loves, until the end of time; and it shall be called by my name.

But if one of us must go first, it is my prayer that it shall be I; for he is strong, I am weak, I am not so necessary to him as he is to me—life without him would not be life; how could I endure it? This prayer is also immortal, and will not cease from being offered up while my race continues. I am the first wife; and in the last wife I shall be repeated.

At Eve's Grave

ADAM: Wheresoever she was, *there* was Eden.

THE END

AFTERWORD

Laura E. Skandera-Trombley

When Samuel Clemens composed *Extracts from Adam's Diary* in the winter of 1892–93, he still possessed what was undoubtedly for him the most important part of his life — his family, consisting of wife Olivia Langdon Clemens and daughters Susy, Clara, and Jean. The Clemenses, after spending the summer in Bad Nauheim, Germany, had moved in the fall of 1892 to the Villa Viviani, just outside Florence, Italy, to reside for the winter. Although it may appear that the family was enjoying a leisurely, well-financed European visit, this extended stay actually signaled the downward spiral that would consume Clemens' last two decades.

In 1891, after a run of bad investments, Clemens left his beloved home of seventeen years at Farmington Avenue in Hartford, Connecticut, and moved his family to Europe in an attempt to cut expenses. Just three years later, in April 1894, he would be forced to declare bankruptcy. The family would remain expatriates until 1900. Although Clemens throughout his professional career was preoccupied with financial remuneration for his creative efforts, during this period he was forced to write in order to keep what remained of his former lifestyle.

When *Extracts from Adam's Diary* was finished, Clemens sent the manuscript to Fred Hall, his manager and partner in the publishing firm Charles L. Webster and Company, and asked him to place it with either *Cosmopolitan* or *Century* magazine. It appeared in neither. A few months later, Clemens wrote again to Hall, implying that perhaps his treatment of the subject matter was a barrier to publication and reassuring Hall that he would rewrite the story in

2 : LAURA E. SKANDERA-TROMBLEY

"a kind of friendly and respectful way that will commend [me] to the Sunday schools."[1] What Clemens did was rewrite the story in a way that would commend him to advertisers.

Instead of appearing in a literary periodical, *Extracts* was published in Irving S. Underhill's *Niagara Book*, a souvenir of the 1893 Buffalo Pan-American Exposition, in a revision that placed the Garden of Eden at Niagara Falls.[2] Clemens was apparently dissatisfied with this commercialized version, because two years later, in 1895, he rewrote the piece yet again, deleting the Niagara Falls references and local allusions.[3] Although he sent the purged manuscript to Harper and Brothers, his new publisher, and asked that it be used in the future, the Niagara version was used for the first book publication in 1904, with added illustrations by Frederick Strothmann (the text of the 1904 edition is the one reproduced here). When Clemens wrote *Eve's Diary* in 1905, he apparently tried again to submit a revised version of *Extracts*, for possible joint publication, again with the Niagara references deleted. On July 17, 1905, he wrote his daughter Clara, "This morning I gutted the old "Adam's Diary" & removed every blemish from it."[4] The next day, Isabel Lyon, his personal secretary, wrote in her daily reminder:

> This afternoon M[r]. Clemens came down stairs with the news that he has revised the Adam's Diary. He read it to me as we sat on the porch, and it is very lovely. He has eliminated the harshnesses — He told me that when he wrote it in Florence years ago that it was literature then, but he was requested to change it — & so he put in things about Niagara Falls & Buffalo to make it an advertisement, & satisfy some man. Adam's recognition of Eve's beauty is very lovely.[5]

Lyon also recorded that "Mr. Clemens wrote Mr. Duneka [an editor at Harper and Brothers] about the correcting of Adam's Diary & the eventual joint publication of Adam's & Eves Diaries."[6] When Duneka received the revised copy, he assured Clemens that his changes would be included in future editions. Despite this exchange of correspondence, when Harper's published "Extracts from Adam's Diary" in *The $30,000 Bequest and Other Stories* in 1906, the 1893 Niagara version was used again.[7] Remarkably, this Oxford edition is the first to publish *Extracts* and *Eve's Diary* in their entirety as a single volume — over ninety years after Clemens initially made the request.

The Niagara version of *Extracts* certainly has its scholarly defenders. Stanley Brodwin finds it "clever" and notes that by placing the first couple in the honeymoon capital, Clemens is able to develop the comical implications of the pun on "fall" throughout the text. Joseph McCullough maintains that by using Niagara Falls as the setting Clemens enhances the "ironic mode" of the story. In the Niagara version, Clemens' waterfall references serve a dual purpose; in addition to humor, as McCullough notes, "theological implications [are derived] from Eve's proscriptions in the park."[8] For instance, when Eve posts a Keep Off the Grass sign, it serves as a foreshadowing of Adam and Eve's eventual expulsion from Eden. The Niagara version's prelapsarian Eve is a joyful, fun-loving innocent, possessing a markedly different personality from the scheming sexual temptress of traditional portrayals. Indeed, at the beginning of *Extracts*, Eve proves an annoyance to Adam. She insists on accompanying him despite his initial desire to be left alone, and because her facility with language is greater than her mate's, she names everything before the slower Adam can utter a single noun.

A critical issue to explore here is why Clemens was so concerned with the content of this piece that he felt compelled to make repeated revisions. *Extracts from Adam's Diary* exemplifies a major personal struggle for Clemens and a concern eventually shared by his family. Was he a serious writer or a wisecracking humorist? Early on in his career, Clemens wrote a letter to his brother Orion in which his insecurity about being perceived as a humorist is evident: "I have had a 'call' to literature, of a low order — i.e., humorous. It is nothing to be proud of, but it is my strongest suit."[9]

Clemens' eldest daughter, Susy, was particularly worried about her father's literary standing. In a letter to family friend Grace King, she states that he "should show himself the great writer that he is, not merely a funny man. Funny! That's all people see in him — a maker of funny speeches!"[10] Whether this humorist/writer conflict was a projection on Clemens' part, or was voiced first by Olivia, then Susy, and subsequently Clemens, it was obviously a serious matter for all of them. The dilemma is suggested by Clemens' struggles with *Extracts*. Without the Niagara references, the piece could not find a publisher; with them, and thus with a decidedly more humorous cast, it was repeatedly published.

Extracts and *Eve's Diary* form part of a group of works Brodwin terms Clemens' "Adamic Diaries."[11] The other texts Brodwin includes in the group are "Passage from Satan's Diary," "Passage from Eve's Diary," "Adam's Soliloquy," and the "Autobiography of Eve," all of which remained unpublished during Clemens' lifetime. While *Extracts* and *Eve's Diary* are overtly humorous in tone and effect, the works published posthumously are bitter and harshly satirical. William Macnaughton notes in *Mark Twain's Last Years as a Writer* that *Extracts* and *Eve's Diary* differ from the rest of the Adamic Diaries because they were written for a general audience that expected vintage, funny "Mark Twain," and claims that they "lack the complexity and pathos of the posthumous diaries."[12] Brodwin describes the Adamic Diaries as "sophisticated folktales" and argues that "they embody a major strand in Twain's complex tapestry of artistic devices, patterns, and 'mythic imagery.' "[13]

Extracts and *Eve's Diary* serve as natural extensions of the dialogue Clemens had begun decades earlier when he satirized the fundamentalist Sunday school images that he was exposed to in his youth. An example that comes immediately to mind is found early on in the pages of *Adventures of Huckleberry Finn* (1885) in Miss Watson's literal interpretation of Matthew 6:6, "But thou, when thou prayest, enter into thy closet." Instead of teaching Huckleberry the differences between hypocritical public displays of piety and private expressions of devotion, Miss Watson takes him into an actual closet for an extended prayer session.

In his second version of *Extracts*, Clemens endows Adam and Eve with realistic character traits while having them enact their mythic roles in Eden/Niagara Falls. He breaks with conventional accounts of original sin with his burlesque of the cause and after-effects of the fall. While traditional biblical interpretations cite Eve's disobedience and hubris, Clemens has Adam claim responsibility and blame humor instead of pride, a passage that has a clearly self-referential note.

[Eve] accuses *me* of being the cause of our disaster! She says, with apparent sincerity and truth, that the Serpent assured her that the forbidden fruit was not apples, it was chestnuts. I said I was innocent, then, for I had not eaten any chestnuts. She said the Serpent informed her that "chestnut" was a figurative term meaning an aged and mouldy joke. I turned pale at that, for I have made many jokes to pass the weary time, and some of them could have been of that sort, thought I had honestly supposed that they were new when I made them. She asked me if I had made one just at the time of the catastrophe. I was obliged to admit that I had made one to myself, though not aloud. It was this. I was thinking about the Falls, and I said to myself, "How wonderful it is to see that vast body of water tumble down there!" Then in an instant a bright thought flashed into my head, and I let it fly, saying, "It would be a deal more wonderful to see it tumble *up* there!" — and I was just about to kill myself with laughing at it when all nature broke loose in war and death and I had to flee for my life. "There," she said with triumph, "that is just it; the Serpent mentioned that very jest, and called it the First Chestnut, and said it was coeval with the creation." Alas, I am indeed to blame. Would that I were not witty; oh, would that I had never had that radiant thought! (51–53)

In the Niagara version of *Extracts from Adam's Diary*, humor proved to be the temptation Clemens himself could not withstand. While composing and revising this piece, he found himself at a personal crossroads: in order to support his family and try to rectify his dismal financial situation, he must play the role that he and his family wished him to abandon; he must be the humorist Mark Twain, "a maker of funny speeches."

Although Clemens found repeated publication with the Niagara version, the critical reception of his text was decidedly unenthusiastic. An anonymous reviewer in 1897 concluded, "In 'Adam's Diary' Mark Twain is at his feeblest and vulgarest; he fell no lower in 'A Yankee at the Court of King Arthur.'"[14] Harry Thurston Peck's 1904 review of the Niagara text was acidic in tone: "There is something unutterably pathetic about a book like Mark Twain's *Extracts from Adam's Diary*. It shows just how far a man who was once a great humorist can fall.”[15] Clemens’ work was treated far more kindly, although ethnocentrically, in an anonymous 1904 review in the *Spectator*:

> Not only is this little book to be acquitted of the charge of any real irreverence, but . . . its audacity is so tempered by delicacy, and even tenderness, of feeling that no broad-minded reader can arise from its perusal without enhanced admiration for the great and kindly humorist who, since Dickinson’s death, has done more than any other writer to promote the gaiety of the two great branches of the Anglo-Saxon race.[16]

In marked contrast to *Extracts*, when *Eve’s Diary* was published by Harper’s in book form in 1906 (the edition reproduced here), it received a much warmer critical reception. Clemens was delighted with the pen-and-ink drawings by Lester Ralph. (*Eve’s Diary* was initially published sans illustrations in the Christmas 1905 issue of *Harper’s Monthly*.) After he was informed that the librarians of Worcester, Massachusetts, had declared the book indecent and removed it from the shelves because of its supposedly pornographic illustrations of a prelapsarian Eve, he wrote a stinging rebuke that was printed in the *Washington (D.C.) Herald*.

> It appears that the pictures in “Eve’s Diary” were first discovered by a lady librarian. When she made the dreadful find, being very careful, she jumped at no hasty conclusions — not she — she examined the horrid things in detail. It took her some time to examine them all, but she did her hateful duty! I don’t blame her for this careful examination; the time spent was, I am sure, enjoyable, for I found considerable fascination in them myself.
>
> Then she took the book to another librarian, a male this time, and he, also, took a long time to examine the unclothed ladies. He must have found something of the same sort of fascination in them that I found.[17]

Clemens wrote *Eve’s Diary* specifically as a companion piece to *Extracts*. While composing it, he took a revised portion of Adam’s diary and transplanted it to Eve’s narrative. In a July 1905 letter to Duneka, he explained, “I wrote Eve’s Diary, she using Adam’s Diary as her (unwitting and unconscious) text, of course, since to use any other text would have been an imbecility."[18] Clemens devised a most fitting plan, considering the subject matter. In his mind *Eve's Diary* was so closely related to *Extracts* that he asked Duneka to "bind Adam and Eve in one cover. They score points against each other—so, if not bound together, some of the points would not be perceived.... P.S. Please send another Adam's Diary, so that I can make two revised copies." In the same letter Clemens concluded, "Eve's Diary is Eve's love-story, but we will not name it that."[19] While *Eve's Diary* is clearly a love story, it also functions as a satire on conventional religion, as well as serving as Clemens' loving eulogy to his deceased wife.

When Clemens was first introduced to Olivia on December 31, 1867, he met a woman who was far better educated than he was. Judging from the contents of personal letters and from her commonplace book, she was in fact a learned woman, well versed in classical and modern American and British literature. Olivia helped Clemens read proof for his first full-length book, *The Innocents Abroad*, and he found her assistance so valuable that he subsequently appointed her editor for all of his books. In a letter to Elizabeth Jordan on March 10, 1905, Clemens reiterated the power of Olivia's influence: "she edited all my manuscripts, beginning this labor of love a year before we were married, continuing it 36 years."[20]

As Olivia won the role of Clemens' first muse, Susy became his second. She grew into an intelligent, introspective young woman, and her father entertained the hope that she might become a writer. After Susy's death in August 1896, although his narrative powers were still strong, Clemens seldom ventured beyond the relatively constricted range of the short story. When Olivia died in June 1904, the one constant in Samuel Clemens' life for the past thirty-six years died as well. With her death, his ability to complete long narratives disappeared entirely. Clemens never recovered from his losses, and significantly, neither did Mark Twain. When Clemens was courting Olivia he wrote her a letter that would prove prophetic in light of the treatment and tone of his future subject matter in the diaries: "what we want is a *home*—we are done with the shows ... of life.... At least *I* am—& 'I' means both of us, & 'both of us' means I of course—for are not we Twain one flesh?"[21]

By the time Clemens began writing *Eve's Diary* in 1905, his life had changed dramatically since the initial composition of *Extracts*. After an around-the-world lecture tour in 1895–96, he was again on solid financial ground and, acting on the advice of Olivia, had repaid his creditors dollar for dollar. But his financial resurrection was overshadowed by Susy's death and Olivia's steadily worsening health. Clemens composed *Eve's Diary* roughly a year after Olivia's death while summering at Dublin, New Hampshire, with his daughter Jean and Isabel Lyon. Despite his grief, he was extraordinarily pleased with his work and often read it out loud to small gatherings of appreciative friends. "Eve's Diary is finished — I've been waiting for her to speak, but she doesn't say anything more," Clemens told Lyon on July 18, 1905.[22]

The narrative structure that Clemens employs in *Eve's Diary* is particularly interesting. Eve begins by telling the story of her creation and goes on to describe her relationship with Adam. At various points in the text Clemens interpolates portions of Adam's diary. After Eve's death at the end of the tale, Clemens allows Adam the last word: "Wheresoever she was, *there* was Eden." This story structure mimics a humorous letter Clemens and Olivia co-wrote to Mary Fairbanks when they were newly married, in which the two display a freewheeling give-and-take and Clemens manages to seize the final word (Olivia's "commentaries" are in parentheses):

> We are settled down & comfortable, & the days swing by with a whir & a flash & are gone, we know not where and scarcely care. . . . But there is no romance in this existence for Livy. (False) . . . And we two will get along well together — I feel it, I know it. We have been married eleven days, & not thirty-five (not one) cross words have passed between us.

In a postscript, the raillery between the two is given free rein:

> How thankful I am that you have some one to interpret my letter for you L.
> It is a sort of grammar that renders interpretation very necessary. S.
> I don't think so-*because* — L.
> And I *do* for the same reason. S.
> *No.* — L.
> Go to bed, Woman! S.

I am not sleepy — L.

This it is to be married. S.

Yes indeed-woe is me! This it *is* to be married L.

Go on-jaw-jaw-jaw. S.

I don't *think* so — L.

Well, *take* the last word. S.[23]

In *Eve's Diary* Clemens was intent on revisiting his happiest moments. The two texts in this volume should be viewed as the culmination of Olivia's influence on his personal beliefs and writing. When Clemens married into the Langdon family, he entered a reformist culture that supported abolition, hydropathic medicine, and women's rights. In a shift neatly coinciding with his engagement, Clemens began to reverse his anti-suffragist views and eventually came to incorporate his wife's feminist beliefs into some of his work, both fiction and nonfiction. By the end of his life, he was considered such an advocate of equal rights for women that activists often enlisted his support for their cause.

This evolution in Clemens' politics is consistently reflected in his post-1870s writings. He deliberately chose subject matter that served as a vehicle for exploring his changing thoughts on gender issues. An example of his defining and then deconstructing rigid gender binaries comes early in *Adventures of Huckleberry Finn*, when Huck disguises himself as a girl and stops at Judith Loftus's home to find out if she has any news about the search for him and Jim. When she tells him that she thinks Jim is still in the area, a frightened Huck takes up needle and thread. After watching him fumble, Mrs. Loftus concludes that Huck is not a girl and devises a series of tests to prove her suspicions: she has Huck throw a lump of lead at a rat and then drops the lump in his skirted lap to see how he catches it. Huck gives scripted "masculine" responses to each of the tests — that is, his throw is accurate and he clamps his legs together.

Clemens has Huck take part in this feminine charade to demonstrate that within contemporary cultural norms being female requires, among other things, restricted movement and a lack of intellectual and physical prowess.

When Mrs. Loftus tells Huck that missing rats is what girls do, she is giving a lesson on gender roles and expectations. She is teaching Huck how the game is played, and the implication is that once he understands the rules, not only can he play but he can win.

Extracts from Adam's Diary and *Eve's Diary* are part of Clemens' continuing dialogue on gender. In *Extracts* it is immediately apparent that Eve is the active force, while Adam is the doubting, reluctant follower. His rather dense attitude is summed up in his repeated entries for Sunday: "Pulled through." Adam duly catalogues Eve's industriousness in organizing their lives, and one senses a growing appreciation on his part for her intelligence and capacity to provide for them. Although Adam affects an emotionally cold, indifferent demeanor, he gradually comes to appreciate and then to rely on and finally to love Eve. With the birth of their first child, Cain, Adam is mystified and initially assumes that the infant is a kind of fish, or later on in its development, perhaps a kangaroo or a bear. By the end of *Extracts*, ten years after the birth of Abel, Adam freely admits he was mistaken about Eve: "it is better to live outside the Garden with her than inside it without her" (89).

Introduced in *Extracts* by her partner, Eve tells her story in her own voice more than a decade later. Clemens' Eve not only speaks and thinks for herself, but she also raises theological issues in questioning her existence. In the course of *Eve's Diary* she develops a keen aesthetic appreciation of her surroundings and ponders existential questions such as the nature of being. Adam, on the other hand, does not. Does this imply, then, that Clemens created a masculine Eve and a feminine Adam? Not at all. Clemens was careful to provide a passage where Eve asks herself why she loves Adam, and answers,

Merely because he is masculine, I think.

At the bottom he is good, and I love him for that, but I could love him without it. (101)

An important part of Eve's role in both works is to humanize Adam, and this too can be seen as a reflection of Clemens' relationship with Olivia. When they were first engaged, he was astounded by her open affection and happily marveled at the endearments she directed toward him. It was Olivia who helped reveal to him how emotionally reserved his childhood had been. After he got used to Olivia's effusiveness, Clemens welcomed the change.

Eve, like Olivia, is not blind to her partner's flaws. In *Eve's Diary* she often protects Adam's self-image: "I do not let him see that I am aware of his defect," she says in reference to Adam's inability to name things (29). Olivia also functioned as Clemens' protector at times. He recognized her generosity of spirit in a letter he wrote shortly after her death, to Susan Crane, Olivia's adopted older sister.

Yes, she did love me; & nothing that I did, no hurt that I inflicted upon her, no tears that I caused those dear eyes to shed, could break it down, or even chill it. It always rose again, it always burned again, as warm & bright as ever. Nothing could wreck it, nothing could extinguish it.[24]

It is not surprising that Clemens undertook fictional and nonfictional explorations of gender, in view of his immediate family's immersion in women's issues for more than three decades.[25] In *Extracts from Adam's Diary* and *Eve's Diary* Clemens was reaching the end of an era of his life, as he was acutely and often painfully aware, and his literary response was to return to the beginning. With Olivia as his wife, he entered a world of fascinating possibility combined with intellectual excitement, a world defined by a deeply held love. Without Olivia and his family circle, he suffered an emotional fall and the eventual loss of his gift for sustained narrative writing. Yet a single well-crafted line can speak volumes, as Adam's last words in *Eve's Diary* did a century ago, and as they do now.

Wheresoever she was, *there* was Eden.

NOTES

1. *Mark Twain's Letters to His Publishers*, Hamlin Hill, ed. (Berkeley: University of California Press, 1967) 356.

2. The other essays included in the *Niagara Book* (Buffalo: Underhill and Nichols, 1893) are "Niagara, First and Last" by W. D. Howells, "What to See" by Frederick Almy, "The Geology of Niagara Falls" by N. S. Shaler, "Famous Visitors at Niagara Falls" by Thomas R. Slicer,

"Historic Niagara" by Peter A. Porter, "The Flora and Fauna of Niagara Falls" by David F. Day, "As It Rushes By" by Edward S. Martin, "The Utilization of Niagara's Power" by Coleman Sellers, and "The Hydraulic Canal" by W. C. Johnson.

3. Joseph B. McCullough, "Mark Twain's First Chestnut: Revisions in 'Extracts from Adam's Diary,'" *Essays in Arts and Sciences* 23 (October 1994): 50.

4. Mark Twain Papers (hereafter cited as MTP), The Bancroft Library, University of California, Berkeley. Mark Twain's previously unpublished words are all © 1996 by Chemical Bank as Trustee of the Mark Twain Foundation, which reserves all reproduction or dramatization rights in every medium. Quotation is made with the permission of the University of California Press and Robert H. Hirst, General Editor, Mark Twain Project. Each of these quotations is identified by a dagger (†) in its citation.

5. Isabel Van Kleek Lyon, July 17, 1905 Daily Reminder, no. 2, MTP.

6. July 16, 1905 Daily Reminder, no. 2, MTP.

7. Indeed, the first publication of the story as Clemens actually intended it took place over a hundred years after its composition, in Howard G. Baetzhold and Joseph B. McCullough's *The Bible According to Mark Twain: Writings on Heaven, Eden, and the Flood* (Athens: University of Georgia Press, 1995).

8. "Mark Twain's First Chestnut" 53.

9. *My Dear Bro: A Letter from Samuel Clemens to His Brother Orion* (Berkeley: Berkeley Albion, 1961) 6–7.

10. Cited in Grace King, *Memories of a Southern Woman of Letters* (1932; reprint, New York: Books for Libraries Press, 1971) 173–74.

11. "The Humor of the Absurd: Mark Twain's Adamic Diaries," *Criticism* 14 (1972): 50.

12. (Columbia: University of Missouri Press, 1979) 219.

13. " 'Extracts from Adam's Diary,' " *The Mark Twain Encyclopedia*, ed. J. R. LeMaster and James D. Wilson (New York: Garland Publishing, 1993) 274.

14. The anonymous critic was reviewing *Tom Sawyer, Detective, As Told by Huck Finn, and Other Stories*, which included "Extracts." *Bookman* (London) 11 (February 1897): 151–52; cited in Thomas Tenney, *Mark Twain: A Reference Guide* (Boston: G. K. Hall, 1977) 26.

15. "Mark Twain at Ebb Tide," *Bookman* (New York) 19 (May 1904): 235–36; cited in Tenney 40.

16. "Mark Twain's Latest," *Spectator* 92 (June 11, 1904): 925–26; cited in Tenney 39.

17. Cited in Peter Stoneley, *Mark Twain and the Feminine Aesthetic* (Cambridge, England: Cambridge University Press, 1992) 107.

18. *Mark Twain's Letters*, ed. Albert Bigelow Paine, 2 vols. (New York: Harper and Brothers, 1917) 2:775.

19. Paine 2:775.

20. MTP. †

21. *Mark Twain's Letters, Volume 3 (1869)*, eds. Victor Fischer and Michael Frank (Berkeley: University of California Press, 1992) 103.

22. 1905 Daily Reminder, no. 2, MTP.

23. *Mark Twain to Mrs. Fairbanks*, ed. Dixon Wecter (San Marino: Huntington Library, 1949) 123–26.

24. July 25, 1904, MTP. †

25. See Laura E. Skandera-Trombley, *Mark Twain in the Company of Women* (Philadelphia: University of Pennsylvania Press, 1994).

FOR FURTHER READING

Laura E. Skandera-Trombley

For more information on Mark Twain's relationship with Olivia and the Langdon family's involvement with women's issues, see Laura E. Skandera-Trombley's *Mark Twain in the Company of Women* (Philadelphia: University of Pennsylvania Press, 1994).

An excellent reference source for writings considered part of Twain's "Adamic Diaries" is J. R. LeMaster and James D. Wilson's *The Mark Twain Encyclopedia* (New York: Garland Publishing, 1993). For useful publishing background on *Extracts from Adam's Diary*, see Joseph B. McCullough's "Mark Twain's First Chestnut: Revisions in 'Extracts from Adam's Diary,'" *Essays in Arts and Sciences* 23 (October 1994): 49–57.

Critical discussions of *Extracts from Adam's Diary* and *Eve's Diary* include Howard G. Baetzhold, Joseph B. McCullough, and Donald Malcolm's "Mark Twain's Eden/Flood Parable: 'The Autobiography of Eve,'" *American Literary Realism* 24, no. 1 (Fall 1991): 23–38; Stanley Brodwin's "The Humor of the Absurd: Mark Twain's Adamic Diaries," *Criticism* 14 (1972): 50–51, "Mark Twain's Masks of Satan: The Final Phase," *American Literature* 45 (May 1973): 206–27, and "The Theology of Mark Twain: Banished Adam and the Bible," in *Critical Essays on Mark Twain: 1910–1980*, ed. Louis J. Budd (Boston: G. K. Hall, 1983) 176–93; Everett Emerson's *The Authentic Mark Twain: A Literary Biography of Samuel L. Clemens* (Philadelphia: University of Pennsylvania Press, 1984); William R. Macnaughton's *Mark Twain's Last Years as a Writer* (Columbia: University of Missouri Press, 1979); and Peter Stoneley's *Mark Twain and the Feminine Aesthetic* (Cambridge, England: Cambridge University Press, 1992).

For major works on Mark Twain and religion, see Allison Ensor's *Mark Twain and the Bible* (Lexington: University of Kentucky Press, 1969); John Q. Hayes' *Mark Twain and Religion: A Mirror of American Eclecticism*, ed. Fred A. Rodewald (New York: Peter Lang, 1989); and *The Bible According to*

Mark Twain: Writings on Heaven, Eden, and the Flood, ed. Howard G. Baetzhold and Joseph B. McCullough (Athens: University of Georgia Press, 1995).

ILLUSTRATORS AND ILLUSTRATIONS

IN MARK TWAIN'S FIRST AMERICAN EDITIONS

Beverly R. David & Ray Sapirstein

From the "gorgeous gold frog" stamped into the cover of *The Celebrated Jumping Frog of Calaveras County* in 1867 to the comet-riding captain on the frontispiece of *Extract from Captain Stormfield's Visit to Heaven* in 1909, illustrators and illustrations were an integral part of Mark Twain's first editions.

Twain marketed most of his major works by subscription, and illustration functioned as an important sales tool. Subscription books were packed with pictures of every type and size and were bound in brassy gold-stamped covers. The books were sold by agents who flipped through a prospectus filled with lively illustrations, selected text, and binding samples. Illustrations quickly conveyed a sense of the story, condensing the proverbial "thousand words" and outlining the scope and tone of the work, making an impression on the potential purchaser even before the full text had been printed. Book canvassers were rewarded with up to 50 percent of the selling price, which started at $3.50 and ranged as high as $7.00 for more ornate bindings. The books themselves were seldom produced until a substantial number of customers had placed orders. To justify the relatively high price and to reassure buyers that they were getting their money's worth, books published by subscription had to offer sensational volume and apparent substance. As Frank Bliss of the American Publishing Company observed, these consumers "would not pay for blank paper and wide margins. They wanted everything filled up with type or pictures." While authors of trade books generally tolerated lighter sales, gratified by attracting a "better class of readers," as Hamlin Hill put it, authors of subscription books sacrificed literary respectability for popular appeal and considerable profit.[1]

The humorist George Ade remembered Twain's books vividly, offering us a child's-eye view of the nineteenth-century subscription book market.

Just when front-room literature seemed at its lowest ebb, so far as the American boy was concerned, along came Mark Twain. His books looked at a distance, just like the other distended, diluted, and altogether tasteless volumes that had been used for several decades to balance the ends of the center table . . . so thick and heavy and emblazoned with gold that [they] could keep company with the bulky and high-priced Bible. . . . The publisher knew his public, so he gave a pound of book for every fifty cents, and crowded in plenty of wood-cuts and stamped the outside with golden bouquets and put in a steel engraving of the author, with a tissue paper veil over it, and "sicked" his multitude of broken-down clergymen, maiden ladies, grass widows, and college students on the great American public.

Can you see the boy, Sunday morning prisoner, approach the book with a dull sense of foreboding, expecting a dose of Tupper's *Proverbial Philosophy*? Can you see him a few minutes later when he finds himself linked arm-in-arm with Mulberry Sellers or Buck Fanshaw or the convulsing idiot who wanted to know if Christopher Columbus was sure-enough dead? No wonder he curled up on the hair-cloth sofa and hugged the thing to his bosom and lost all interest in Sunday school. *Innocents Abroad* was the most enthralling book ever printed until *Roughing It* appeared. Then along came *The Gilded Age*, *Life on the Mississippi*, and *Tom Sawyer*. . . . While waiting for a new one we read the old ones all over again.[2]

Publishers, editors, and Twain himself spent a good deal of time on design — choosing the most talented artists, directing their interpretations of text, selecting from the final prints, and at times removing material they deemed unfit for illustration.[3]

With the exception of *Following the Equator* (1897), books released in the twilight of Twain's career were not sold by subscription. Twain's later books, published for the trade market by Harper and Brothers, seldom contained more than a frontispiece and a dozen or so tasteful illustrations, rather than the hundreds of illustrations per volume that subscription publishing demanded. Illustration, however, remained a major component of Twain's later work in two important cases: *Extracts from Adam's Diary*, illustrated by Fred

Strothmann in 1904, and *Eve's Diary*, illustrated by Lester Ralph in 1906.

The stories behind the illustrators and illustrations of Mark Twain's first editions abound in back-room intrigue. The besotted or negligent lapses of some of the artists and the procrastinations of the engravers are legendary. The consequent production delays, mistimed releases, and copyright infringements all implied a lack of competent supervision that frequently infuriated Twain and ultimately encouraged him to launch his own publishing company.

In many cases, Twain took illustrations into account as he wrote and edited his text, using them as counterpoint and accompaniment to his words, often allowing them to inform his general narrative strategy and to influence the amount of detail he felt necessary to include in his written descriptions. In the most artful and carefully considered illustrated works, an analysis of the relationships between author and illustrator and between text and pictures illuminates key dimensions of Twain's writings and the responses they have elicited from readers. Examinations of even the most straightforward examples of decorative imagery yield insights into the publishing history of Twain's books and his attitudes toward the production process.

The original illustrations in Twain's works have often been replaced in the twentieth century by subsequent visual interpretations. But while Norman Rockwell's well-known nostalgic renderings of *Tom Sawyer* and *Huckleberry Finn* may tell us much about 1930s sensibilities, we would do well to reacquaint ourselves with the first American editions and the artwork they contained if we want to understand the books Twain wrote and the world they affected.

Illustrated books, like the illustrated weekly magazines that first appeared in the 1860s, were a significant source of visual images entering nineteenth-century homes. Because of their widespread popularity and the relative paucity of other sources of visual information, Twain's books helped to define America's perceptions of remote people, exotic scenes, and historic events. In addition to being an essential element of Mark Twain's body of work, illustrations are a documentary source in their own right, a window into Twain's world and our own.

NOTES

1. For background on subscription book publishing, see Hamlin Hill, *Mark Twain and Elisha Bliss* (Columbia: University of Missouri Press, 1964), chapter 1. See also R. Kent Rasmussen, "Subscription-book publishing" entry, *Mark Twain A to Z: The Essential Reference to His Life and Writings* (New York: Facts on File, 1995), p. 448.

2. George Ade, "Mark Twain and the Old-Time Subscription Book," *Review of Reviews* 61 (June 10, 1910): 703–4; reprinted in Frederick Anderson, ed., *Mark Twain: The Critical Heritage* (London: Routledge and Kegan Paul, 1971), pp. 337–39.

3. Beverly R. David, *Mark Twain and His Illustrators, Volume 1 (1869–1875)* (Troy, N.Y.: Whitston Publishing Company, 1986), discusses in detail Twain's involvement in the production of his early books.

READING THE ILLUSTRATIONS IN

EXTRACTS FROM ADAM'S DIARY AND *EVE'S DIARY*

Ray Sapirstein

With an image to complement each page of text, *Extracts from Adam's Diary* (1904) and *Eve's Diary* (1906) were unique among Mark Twain's works in giving words and illustrations equal emphasis. The illustrations offered decorative accompaniment, and along with very wide margins and heavy paper, they transformed otherwise thin volumes into full-sized books.

These design features were common among the gift books in vogue during the late nineteenth and early twentieth centuries. Such volumes were usually slim, elaborately decorated editions of previously published texts and were often produced for sale during the holiday season — collections of short stories or poetry organized in brief independent segments to be nibbled at for entertainment rather than devoured in large gulps. Filling the same niche at the turn of the century as coffee-table books do today, gift books ordinarily treated pleasant subjects and light themes, offering charm, amusement, and packaged sentiment.

While both *Adam's Diary* and *Eve's Diary* nominally satisfied the gift book formula, Twain's characteristic irony and subject matter significantly stretched the boundaries of the genre. In the seemingly innocuous guise of the gift book format, Twain parodied Genesis and its "old chestnuts," the traditional parables of creation, original sin, and Eve's responsibility for the fall of humanity.

Frederick Strothmann (1879–1958) and Lester Ralph (1877–1927) each employed a consciously crafted graphic primitivism to convey the idyllic innocence of Eden. Strothmann's clever faux-Egyptian hieroglyphic tablets in *Adam's Diary* mitigated Twain's pointed ironies with a cheerful cuteness that presaged the style of many twentieth-century cartoons. Following Twain's text, Strothmann employed technological anachronism as his major comic device: he presented Eve using a washboard and Adam smoking cigars, and inscribed his tablets with suitcases, easy chairs, clock towers, and so on. In style and subject matter, his portrayal of a modern Stone Age family calls to mind *The Flintstones*, the animated television series that first aired in the 1960s and inspired innumerable variants in cartoons and contemporary advertising.

Rather spare by gift book standards, Strothmann's cover for *Adam's Diary*, a modification of the frontispiece, was printed in color on Harper's standard-issue red cloth. It presented a peach-colored Adam clothed in a leafy green toga. Eve and the rest of the animals in the frontispiece do not appear on the cover; only two gray monkeys look on as Adam chisels a tablet.

An artist for *Harper's Weekly*, Strothmann also illustrated other books by Twain, including a 1903 edition of the jumping frog story and a 1905 collection of previously published sketches, *Editorial Wild Oats*, as well as books by Carolyn Wells, Ellis Parker Butler, and Lucille Gulliver.[1] Harper and Brothers originally enlisted him to do the illustrations for *Eve's Diary*, but Twain specified that he wanted an artist with a more refined approach, and Lester Ralph was selected. An accomplished painter, illustrator, and etcher, Ralph was trained at the Art Students League in New York, the Slade School in London, and the Académie Julien in Paris. He had covered the 1897 Turko-Greek and 1898–1902 South African Wars as an artist-correspondent, and he later illustrated *The Circular Staircase* (1908), by Mary Roberts Rinehart.[2]

Ralph's illustrations in *Eve's Diary* function as a more sophisticated accompaniment to Twain's words than Strothmann's in *Adam's Diary*, adding several significant interpretive dimensions beyond the scope of the text. Unlike Strothmann's comic tablet motif, Lester Ralph's fine-art line drawings present the first couple's nudity directly, with little evasion. Although the figures sparked considerable controversy, they were comparatively minor elements of many of the images, often overshadowed by Ralph's nostalgic paean to Nature in its pristine state, the luxuriant and carefully wrought pastoral landscapes and flora of Eden. Choosing to keep strategic cropping to a minimum, Ralph generally rendered the figures at full length and placed them at a distance within the landscape, precluding graphic anatomical detail. His treatment of the subject was masterful, neither compromising the quality of the images nor corrupting the uninhibited freedom of Eden with obvious artifice. Even for their time, the illustrations were demure and tasteful, legitimated by the archetypal innocence of Eden and the "noble" and contemplative fine-art poses of the figures.

In 1880, twenty-five years before Twain elected to include Ralph's illustrations in *Eve's Diary*, he outlined his thoughts on nudity in art in a discussion of the Old Masters in chapter 50 of *A Tramp Abroad*. Twain attacked the uncritical adulation of images valued primarily for their patina of antiquity and their place in the European high-art tradition, in the process challenging hypocritical Victorian attitudes toward nudity. Even as he railed against Titian's *Venus*, calling it "the foulest, the vilest, the obscenest picture the world possesses," he distinguished nudity from explicit sexuality: "there are pictures of nude women which suggest no impure thought — I am well aware of that." Ridiculing the nineteenth-century bowdlerization of classical sculpture, he wrote,

It makes the body ooze sarcasm at every pore, to go about Rome and Florence and see what this last generation has been doing with the statues. These works, which had stood in innocent nakedness for ages, are all fig-leaved now. . . . Nobody noticed their nakedness before, perhaps: nobody can help noticing it now, the fig-leaf makes it so conspicuous. . . . yet these ridiculous creatures have been thoughtfully and conscientiously fig-leaved by this fastidious generation.

Explaining that a straightforward description of Titian's painting would itself be obscene, Twain commented sarcastically,

It isn't that she is naked and stretched out upon a bed — no, it is the attitude of one of her arms and her hand. If I ventured to describe that attitude, there would be a fine howl — but there the Venus lies . . . and there she has a right to lie, for she is a work of art, and Art has its privileges.

As for scenes of graphic violence — "hideous pictures of blood, carnage, putrefaction" — Twain complained of the disparate moral standards that were applied to art and literature.

But suppose a literary artist ventured to go into a pains-taking and elaborate description of one of these grisly things — the critics would skin him alive. Well let it go, it cannot be helped; Art retains her privileges, Literature has lost hers.[3]

Perhaps seeking to equalize the standards in art and literature and to provide a model of "innocent nakedness," Twain introduced nudity into his work in the safest possible context, utilizing the biblical "fact" of the first couple's nudity and Ralph's high-minded artistic style to stretch the limits of Victorian prudishness. The nudity before the Fall in *Eve's Diary* was of course established in Genesis. Twain thus laid a trap for the committees of decency he so mocked, his joke: to denounce nudity in *Eve's Diary* was to contradict the Bible. He created problems for self-righteous critics by placing both of his likely moral irritants — biblical revisionism and nudity — into direct confrontation with each other. In 1913, after Twain's death, the critic John Macy took delight in Twain's ironic game in *Eve's Diary*.

It is a joke, of course; the absent-minded brontosaurus is there to prove it, and the respectable American librarians and trustees, who (owing to their lack of historical knowledge) objected to Eve's costume and ruled the book off the shelves, made the joke a perfect torture of hilarity.[4]

As Laura Skandera-Trombley mentions in the afterword in this volume, the librarians in Worcester, Massachusetts, were certainly unaware of Twain's irony as they banished the book.

More importantly, perhaps, Ralph's graphic style complements the theme of lost innocence and the multilayered nostalgia the book projects. Twain concludes with Adam's remembering Eve with a dramatic sigh, and the very concept of Eden before the Fall is the archetypal template for nostalgia in western thought. At a time when photographic halftone processes had become the standard technology of the publishing industry, Ralph's precise and elemental line drawings resemble wood engravings and woodcuts, technologies developed along with the printing press centuries before the industrial age. As reaction to industrialism and mass production solidified in the late nineteenth century, handmade articles and handicraft became fashionable, and hand-engraved illustration, in a style much like Ralph's, lingered long after its technological obsolescence.

The arts and crafts movement promoted by the English visionaries John Ruskin and William Morris in the last half of the nineteenth century was a semi-utopian sociopolitical movement that idealized the moral benefits of handicraft and the medieval guild system. American designers, including Louis Comfort Tiffany, the decorator of Twain's home in Hartford — and apparently Lester Ralph — were influenced by the movement and the associated art nouveau and craftsman design styles. Drawing on medieval stained-glass and graphic design, art nouveau also incorporated various non-western design motifs, such as the minimal elegance and shallow surface of Japanese composition. Foremost, art nouveau emphasized detailed organic forms within the composition, familiar to most of us in the designs of Tiffany's famous lamps. In theory, introducing organic, hand-crafted forms into the home would counteract the sterility of mass-produced goods and uplift industrial urban civilization by reintegrating the beauty of the natural world into daily life.

Ralph's illustrations embody several of these design elements: they are heavily outlined, minimally shaded, and graphically two-dimensional, and like Japanese prints, they are vertically oriented landscapes. As such, they imply a subtle revision of the traditional tale of the Fall and exile from Eden, a revision in which industrialization is the agent of corruption and preindustrial society is humankind's ideal natural state. To an extent, the illustrations in *Eve's Diary* suggest a contradiction: Twain's antipathy to medievalism and fascination with technology make him an unlikely promoter of arts and crafts ideals.

The cover of *Eve's Diary* presented no indication of the book's alleged indecencies. Printed on red cloth in green and black ink, a stylized, graphic apple appears at center, an apple tree at lower right. Merely decorative at first glance, the cover facetiously labels the book a forbidden fruit, luring unwary readers into lapse and skepticism. Considering its brevity and picture-book simplicity, *Eve's Diary* is all the more remarkable, its full scope revealed with the integral participation of illustrations that are well executed, decorative, and ultimately challenging.

NOTES

1. Strothmann entry, Theodore Bolton, *American Book Illustrators: A Bibliographic Checklist of 123 Artists* (New York: R. R. Bowker, 1938).

2. See R. Kent Rasmussen, "Ralph, Lester" entry, *Mark Twain A to Z: The Essential Reference to His Life and Writings* (New York: Facts on File, 1995), p. 386; and Ralph's obituary in *American Art Annual* (Washington, D.C.: American Federation of Arts, 1927), 24:345.

3. *A Tramp Abroad*, The Oxford Mark Twain (New York: Oxford University Press, 1996), pp. 577–79.

4. John Macy, chapter on Twain, in *The Spirit of American Literature* (New York: Boni and Liveright, 1913), pp. 248–77; reprinted in Frederick Anderson, ed., *Mark Twain: The Critical Heritage* (London: Routledge and Kegan Paul, 1971), p. 325.

A NOTE ON THE TEXT

Robert H. Hirst

The text of *Extracts from Adam's Diary, Translated from the Original MS* is a photographic facsimile of a copy of the first American edition dated 1904 on the title page. Although books printed from first edition plates were manufactured until at least 1914, the earliest copies of the first edition were published in April 1904. Two copies were deposited with the Copyright Office on April 7 (*BAL* 3480). ■ The text of *Eve's Diary, Translated from the Original MS* is a photographic facsimile of a copy of the first American edition dated 1906 on the title page. Although books printed from first edition plates were manufactured until at least 1914, the earliest copies of the first edition were published in June 1906. Two copies were deposited with the Copyright Office on June 6 (*BAL* 3489). ■ Both of the original volumes reproduced here are in the collection of the Mark Twain House in Hartford, Connecticut (810/C625ext/ 1904/c. 2 and 810/C625ev/1906/c. 1).

THE MARK TWAIN HOUSE

The Mark Twain House is a museum and research center dedicated to the study of Mark Twain, his works, and his times. The museum is located in the nineteen-room mansion in Hartford, Connecticut, built for and lived in by Samuel L. Clemens, his wife, and their three children, from 1874 to 1891. The Picturesque Gothic-style residence, with interior design by the firm of Louis Comfort Tiffany and Associated Artists, is one of the premier examples of domestic Victorian architecture in America. Clemens wrote *Adventures of Huckleberry Finn*, *The Adventures of Tom Sawyer*, *A Connecticut Yankee in King Arthur's Court*, *The Prince and the Pauper*, and *Life on the Mississippi* while living in Hartford.

The Mark Twain House is open year-round. In addition to tours of the house, the educational programs of the Mark Twain House include symposia, lectures, and teacher training seminars that focus on the contemporary relevance of Twain's legacy. Past programs have featured discussions of literary censorship with playwright Arthur Miller and writer William Styron; of the power of language with journalist Clarence Page, comedian Dick Gregory, and writer Gloria Naylor; and of the challenges of teaching *Adventures of Huckleberry Finn* amidst charges of racism.

Beverly R. David is professor emerita of humanities and theater at Western Michigan University in Kalamazoo. She is currently working on volume 2 of *Mark Twain and His Illustrators*, and on a Mark Twain mystery entitled *Murder at the Matterhorn*. She has written a number of sections on illustration for the *Mark Twain Encyclopedia* and her *Mark Twain and His Illustrators, Volume 1 (1869–1875)* was published in 1989. Dr. David resides in Allegan, Michigan, in the summer and Green Valley, Arizona, in the winter.

Shelley Fisher Fishkin, professor of American Studies and English at the University of Texas at Austin, is the author of the award-winning books *Was Huck Black? Mark Twain and African-American Voices* (1993) and *From Fact to Fiction: Journalism and Imaginative Writing in America* (1985). Her most recent book is *Lighting Out for the Territory: Reflections on Mark Twain and American Culture* (1996). She holds a Ph.D. in American Studies from Yale University, has lectured on Mark Twain in Belgium, England, France, Israel, Italy, Mexico, the Netherlands, and Turkey, as well as throughout the United States, and is president-elect of the Mark Twain Circle of America.

Robert H. Hirst is the General Editor of the Mark Twain Project at The Bancroft Library, University of California in Berkeley. Apart from that, he has no other known eccentricities.

Ursula K. Le Guin was born in 1929 in Berkeley, California, where she grew up. Her parents were the anthropologist Alfred Kroeber and the writer Theodora Kroeber, author of *Ishi*. She has written poetry and fiction all her life. Her first publications were poems, and in the 1960s she began to publish short stories and novels. She writes in various modes including realistic fiction, science fiction, fantasy, young children's books, books for young adults, screenplays, essays, verbal texts for musicians, and voice-texts for performance or recording. She has published over eighty short stories, two collections of essays, four volumes of poetry, and sixteen novels. Among the honors her writing has received are a National Book Award, five Hugo and four Nebula Awards, a Kafka Award, a Pushcart Prize, and the Howard Vursell Award of the American Academy of Arts and Letters. She lives in Portland, Oregon, with her husband, Charles A. Le Guin, a historian.

Ray Sapirstein is a doctoral student in the American Civilization Program at the University of Texas at Austin. He curated the 1993 exhibition *Another Side of Huckleberry Finn: Mark Twain and Images of African Americans* at the Harry Ransom Humanities Research Center at the University of Texas at Austin. He is currently completing a dissertation on the photographic illustrations in several volumes of Paul Laurence Dunbar's poetry.

Laura E. Skandera-Trombley, associate professor of English and assistant provost at the State University of New York at Potsdam, holds a Ph.D. in English from the University of Southern California. She is executive director of the Northeast Modern Language Association, and executive coordinator of the Mark Twain Circle of America, and she has lectured on Twain around the world. She became involved in Twain studies in 1987 after discovering the "Clara Letters," a monumental literary find of one hundred letters from Twain to his daughters. Her books include *Epistemology: Turning Points in the History of Poetic Knowledge* (1986), *Mark Twain in the Company of Women* (1994), which *Choice* magazine selected as one of the outstanding academic books of 1995, and three forthcoming publications, *The Woman Who Loved Mark Twain: The Intimate Writings of Isabel Lyon*, *Critical Essays on Maxine Hong Kingston*, and *New Directions in Mark Twain Scholarship*.

ACKNOWLEDGMENTS

There are a number of people without whom The Oxford Mark Twain would not have happened. I am indebted to Laura Brown, senior vice president and trade publisher, Oxford University Press, for suggesting that I edit an "Oxford Mark Twain," and for being so enthusiastic when I proposed that it take the present form. Her guidance and vision have informed the entire undertaking.

Crucial as well, from the earliest to the final stages, was the help of John Boyer, executive director of the Mark Twain House, who recognized the importance of the project and gave it his wholehearted support.

My father, Milton Fisher, believed in this project from the start and helped nurture it every step of the way, as did my stepmother, Carol Plaine Fisher. Their encouragement and support made it all possible. The memory of my mother, Renée B. Fisher, sustained me throughout.

I am enormously grateful to all the contributors to The Oxford Mark Twain for the effort they put into their essays, and for having been such fine, collegial collaborators. Each came through, just as I'd hoped, with fresh insights and lively prose. It was a privilege and a pleasure to work with them, and I value the friendships that we forged in the process.

In addition to writing his fine afterword, Louis J. Budd provided invaluable advice and support, even going so far as to read each of the essays for accuracy. All of us involved in this project are greatly in his debt. Both his knowledge of Mark Twain's work and his generosity as a colleague are legendary and unsurpassed.

Elizabeth Maguire's commitment to The Oxford Mark Twain during her time as senior editor at Oxford was exemplary. When the project proved to be more ambitious and complicated than any of us had expected, Liz helped make it not only manageable, but fun. Assistant editor Elda Rotor's wonderful help in coordinating all aspects of The Oxford Mark Twain, along with literature editor T. Susan Chang's enthusiastic involvement with the project in its final stages, helped bring it all to fruition.

I am extremely grateful to Joy Johannessen for her astute and sensitive copyediting, and for having been such a pleasure to work with. And I appreciate the conscientiousness and good humor with which Kathy Kuhtz Campbell heroically supervised all aspects of the set's production. Oxford president Edward Barry, vice president and editorial director Helen McInnis, marketing director Amy Roberts, publicity director Susan Rotermund, art director David Tran, trade editorial, design and production manager Adam Bohannon, trade advertising and promotion manager Woody Gilmartin, director of manufacturing Benjamin Lee, and the entire staff at Oxford were as supportive a team as any editor could desire.

The staff of the Mark Twain House provided superb assistance as well. I would like to thank Marianne Curling, curator, Debra Petke, education director, Beverly Zell, curator of photography, Britt Gustafson, assistant director of education, Beth Ann McPherson, assistant curator, and Pam Collins, administrative assistant, for all their generous help, and for allowing us to reproduce books and photographs from the Mark Twain House collection. One could not ask for more congenial or helpful partners in publishing.

G. Thomas Tanselle, vice president of the John Simon Guggenheim Memorial Foundation, and an expert on the history of the book, offered essential advice about how to create as responsible a facsimile edition as possible. I appreciate his very knowledgeable counsel.

I am deeply indebted to Robert H. Hirst, general editor of the Mark Twain Project at The Bancroft Library in Berkeley, for bringing his outstanding knowledge of Twain editions to bear on the selection of the books photographed for the facsimiles, for giving generous assistance all along the way, and for providing his meticulous notes on the text. The set is the richer for his advice. I would also like to express my gratitude to the Mark Twain Project, not only for making texts and photographs from their collection available to us, but also for nurturing Mark Twain studies with a steady infusion of matchless, important publications.

I would like to thank Jeffrey Kaimowitz, curator of the Watkinson Library at Trinity College, Hartford (where the Mark Twain House collection is kept), along with his colleagues Peter Knapp and Alesandra M. Schmidt, for having been instrumental in Robert Hirst's search for first editions that could be safely reproduced. Victor Fischer, Harriet Elinor Smith, and especially Kenneth M. Sanderson, associate editors with the Mark Twain Project, reviewed the note on the text in each volume with cheerful vigilance. Thanks are also due to Mark Twain Project associate editor Michael Frank and administrative assistant Brenda J. Bailey for their help at various stages.

I am grateful to Helen K. Copley for granting permission to publish photographs in the Mark Twain Collection of the James S. Copley Library in La Jolla, California, and to Carol Beales and Ron Vanderhye of the Copley Library for making my research trip to their institution so productive and enjoyable.

Several contributors — David Bradley, Louis J. Budd, Beverly R. David, Robert Hirst, Fred Kaplan, James S. Leonard, Toni Morrison, Lillian S. Robinson, Jeffrey Rubin-Dorsky, Ray Sapirstein, and David L. Smith — were particularly helpful in the early stages of the project, brainstorming about the cast of writers and scholars who could make it work. Others who participated in that process were John Boyer, James Cox, Robert Crunden, Joel Dinerstein, William Goetzmann, Calvin and Maria Johnson, Jim Magnuson, Arnold Rampersad, Siva Vaidhyanathan, Steve and Louise Weinberg, and Richard Yarborough.

Kevin Bochynski, famous among Twain scholars as an "angel" who is gifted at finding methods of making their research run more smoothly, was helpful in more ways than I can count. He did an outstanding job in his official capacity as production consultant to The Oxford Mark Twain, supervising the photography of the facsimiles. I am also grateful to him for having put me in touch via e-mail with Kent Rasmussen, author of the magisterial *Mark Twain A to Z*, who was tremendously helpful as the project proceeded, sharing insights on obscure illustrators and other points, and generously being "on call" for all sorts of unforeseen contingencies.

I am indebted to Siva Vaidhyanathan of the American Studies Program of the University of Texas at Austin for having been such a superb research assistant. It would be hard to imagine The Oxford Mark Twain without the benefit of his insights and energy. A fine scholar and writer in his own right, he was crucial to making this project happen.

Georgia Barnhill, the Andrew W. Mellon Curator of Graphic Arts at the American Antiquarian Society in Worcester, Massachusetts, Tom Staley, director of the Harry Ransom Humanities Research Center at the University of Texas at Austin, and Joan Grant, director of collection services at the Elmer Holmes Bobst Library of New York University, granted us access to their collections and assisted us in the reproduction of several volumes of The Oxford Mark Twain. I would also like to thank Kenneth Craven, Sally Leach, and Richard Oram of the Harry Ransom Humanities Research Center for their help in making HRC materials available, and Jay and John Crowley, of Jay's Publishers Services in Rockland, Massachusetts, for their efforts to photograph the books carefully and attentively.

I would like to express my gratitude for the grant I was awarded by the University Research Institute of the University of Texas at Austin to defray some of the costs of researching The Oxford Mark Twain. I am also grateful to American Studies director Robert Abzug and the University of Texas for the computer that facilitated my work on this project (and to UT systems analyst Steve Alemán, who tried his best to repair the damage when it crashed). Thanks also to American Studies administrative assistant Janice Bradley and graduate coordinator Melanie Livingston for their always generous and thoughtful help.

The Oxford Mark Twain would not have happened without the unstinting, wholehearted support of my husband, Jim Fishkin, who went way beyond the proverbial call of duty more times than I'm sure he cares to remember as he shared me unselfishly with that other man in my life, Mark Twain. I am also grateful to my family — to my sons Joey and Bobby, who cheered me on all along the way, as did Fannie Fishkin, David Fishkin, Gennie Gordon, Mildred Hope Witkin, and Leonard, Gillis, and Moss

Plaine — and to honorary family member Margaret Osborne, who did the same.

My greatest debt is to the man who set all this in motion. Only a figure as rich and complicated as Mark Twain could have sustained such energy and interest on the part of so many people for so long. Never boring, never dull, Mark Twain repays our attention again and again and again. It is a privilege to be able to honor his memory with The Oxford Mark Twain.

Shelley Fisher Fishkin
Austin, Texas
April 1996